Also by Thomas F. Cook

Novels
Blooming
Illyria

Plays
A Score of Zero In Tennis
The Chicken Screamer
Victoria's Children
The Cigar Tree
Lost Dogs
The gAy-List
The Day Job
Like Being In Love
Side Effects
A Tendency To Say Ummm
The Names Have Been Changed

Other Work
The Family Of Charles Abby Cook

Miss Over

by

Thomas F. Cook

First published by Diamond C Press
www.diamondcpress.com

This is a work of fiction. Events and situations in the book
are purely fictional. Any resemblance to actual persons,
living or dead, is coincidental.

Printed in The United States of America.

ISBN: 0990720608
ISBN-13: 978-0-9907206-0-7

Author photo courtesy of Emma Lumsden.
Cover photo: *Griqualand, 2012,* by the author.
Back cover photo: Anonymous, Italian, *Leda And The
Swan,* ca. 1550 - 1580, Metropolitan Museum of Art.

Acknowledgments:

The Writers Room, NY and Paragraph, NY. My writing group Paratactic: Bonnie Altucher, Jenna Leigh Evans, Rosalie Necht, Roberta Newman, and Helen Terndrup. I would also like to thank Dina Montes, Andreas Guido Verras, John Delk, Pedro de Armas-Kendall, and a playwright and teacher who died in the 80s, but whose kindness and encouragement I still have with me: Meade Roberts. For the Khoi stories, I was inspired and borrowed heavily from the work of Wilhelm Bleek and Lucy Lloyd. In particular their work: *Specimens of Bushmen Folklore*.

A note about the animals

All of the animal behavior is based on what I witnessed and what I was told by guides. It is not meant to be perfectly accurate. For example, one of the guides told our group that hyenas will dig up human corpses and eat them. This is not true. However, because the animals make Rebecca think that her own actions are on display or on trial, I wasn't looking for "animal accuracy" but rather the mix of truth and fiction that we use to understand ourselves and the world.

The Okavango Delta

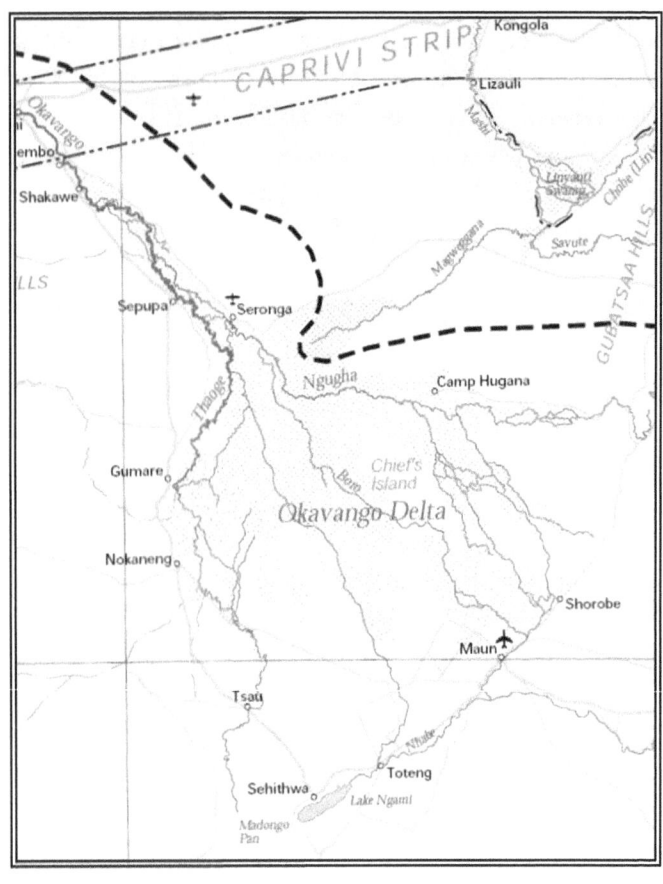

Chapter 1

In transit

She woke to the sound of a call. An electronic *ping* cut through the stiff dry air and brought her back to life, though she hadn't actually been sleeping. She had only been pretending to sleep, thinking that if she aped the other passengers she would eventually slip into some form of rest before their arrival in South Africa.

Though Rebecca was 46, she had never been on a flight longer than ninety minutes and hadn't any idea of how difficult it would be to sit – *just sit* – for fourteen hours. Julian, her best friend, had warned her, but she hadn't imagined it could be as horrible as it had been so far. The flight was packed — every seat taken — and now, halfway across the ocean, they were expected to close their eyes and sleep in that awkward sitting position bound by a seat belt across the waist. She had absolutely no idea how all the other people were able to do it.

A flight attendant brushed lightly against Rebecca's arm as she made her way up the aisle to attend to whoever had summoned her at this quiet hour. Perhaps it was an accident. Maybe a hefty fellow, shifting in his sleep to get more comfortable, unknowingly pressed with his hip the little white button with the silhouette of a short skirted woman. Rebecca pressed down on the arm rests, lifted herself gently, trying not to disturb the man to her right, and looked over the rows ahead of her. She saw only the tops of heads poking over identical seats. Some bald. Some gray. Brunettes. Blondes. All sleeping. Only one head retained a tiny white pillow. They looked like the coins in the muscular dystrophy card they used to have standing on the counter at her dry cleaner's. Halves of heads. Tips of tails.

She watched with a smile as the young woman gracefully made her way up the aisle, unhurried — lightly touching the seats behind the dormant heads — as if she was a saint blessing the soon to be resurrected. *She walks on air*, Rebecca thought. *She is a woman who walks on air.*

She looked for the light switch on her armrest and turned it on, hoping the light would not bother anyone, especially the rather amiable man sitting to her right who had introduced himself as Trevor Wardman. After a brief pause, light splashed down on her in a bright cone, but it seemed not to disturb Trevor. She retrieved her backpack from under the seat in front of her and looked for something to read. She had two things: a book of poems and a gossip magazine. She didn't know why she bought the magazine and she was too preoccupied to read poetry, but she chose the book of poems anyway and opened randomly to one:

Sister sniffs the poison flower —
Then bows to pink its thorny stem —
She plants the flower — in her hair —
And dubs the flower — diadem.

No no no. Not now, she thought. She put it away. For something to do and feeling a grin work its way onto her face, she pulled from her pack a magnifying glass that she always carried in case she wanted to observe something, like a wildflower or a bug in the woods, or the increasingly rare postage stamp. This time she decided to use it to inspect her neighbor's scalp.

Trevor was a South African who was working on some sort of reality television show about a South African orphanage that would be "shown in America, cross thumbs," he had said. He was affable and an enthusiastic talker, but she noticed even before they took off from JFK in New York that he had the most God-awful breath she had ever encountered — something that had to have been caused by an ulcer or a chronic stomach condition. While he talked about his business (she could remember almost nothing of what he had said about it) she had held her breath and took sporadic gasps of air while he was looking down and cutting the tiny piece of meat that they called Beef Wellington. It amused her though. She was not easily put off by such things as bad breath.

She looked around to see if anyone was awake or watching her. No one was. She took her glass and peered at the crown of his head, hoping to see some dandruff or a blemish. But there was nothing. His scalp was white and clean and each black hair of his head plunged into a pore of its own. *What a jungle*, she thought, *and no thinning either*. That brought to mind an awful fight she had with Julian not too long ago and she thought about it after tucking her glass into the seat pocket.

It was a simple mistake really. It was a Friday night and he had picked her up on their way to Sushi Rock in downtown

Cleveland. When she got in the car, something about the car's overhead light and the tilt of his head made it apparent that he was just starting to thin at the crown, and she said, before thinking better of it, "Julian, is your hair finally starting to thin?"

"What," he said, but it wasn't a question and she could tell he was already defensive.

"Nothing," Rebecca said, "I just thought... it looked... ummm... like it was thinning, but probably not."

"I'm not losing my hair Rebecca. My grandfather had a full head of hair when he died and it'll be exactly the same for me. It's the mother's father. That's the hair that boys get."

"It must have been the light."

"Of course it was. I have a full head of beautiful blond hair and a great ass. That's what my mother always said to me." He laughed and added, "What kind of mother says that?"

She was relieved that Julian had laughed as he pulled onto Abbe Road and that he hadn't stayed defensive. He was very good at getting over things and moving on. She sometimes thought it was one of his gifts; at least he was much better at it than she was. But then her problems were so much more difficult to get over — things you couldn't talk about in the festive atmosphere of a sushi restaurant with a large tray of tuna, salmon and yellowtail maki in front of you.

She looked around the dark cabin again, almost hoping someone else would be awake. No one stirred. She couldn't even hear a slightly choked snore.

In a way Julian was the reason she was taking this trip. Ever since they had rented the movie *Out of Africa* a few years ago, they had played a silly game he had started about the line, "I had a farm in Africa." They would repeat it to each other in many different ways, as dramatically as possible, using fake British or Danish accents.

"Oh Rebecca *dear*," he would say, "I had a dog in Africa but it was run over by a Land Rover."

"Oh Julian *darling*," she would return, "I had a car in Africa but it was crushed by a mad elephant."

And then, "I read a book in Africa but I went blind before I reached the ending."

"Why who do you think you are, darling, Milton?"

They would go on this way, and eventually, always, degenerate into vulgarity — "I had a puke in Africa," "I had a piss in Africa," "I took a dump in Africa," "I had a fuck in Africa."

But after awhile, especially over the last year, the game had changed for Rebecca and by the time her father got sick, taking an African safari was something she desperately wanted to do. She needed this trip.

Chapter 2

It had been a terrible year. It began when she realized at the depressingly early age of 44 that she was entering menopause. In and of itself, the menopause didn't trouble her — it was something about having to let go. It made her think about her old girlfriends, the friends she'd had in her twenties when she was going through what she called her "promiscuous" stage. She supposed that most people would find it hard to believe that she had enjoyed a promiscuous stage, and promiscuous in Illyria could hardly be the same thing as promiscuous in a large city like Cleveland, but it was, nevertheless, one of the stages of her life. Menopause made her look back on it, and the three good friends she had at the time: Joanne, Molly and Shannon. All three had all married and pursued the life of husband and children while she... she grew closer to Julian.

Julian was ten years younger than she was and he had a cute, winsome kind of expression that was well-suited to his job teaching fifth graders. They had met in a bar in downtown Illyria, of all the strange places, and they had hit it off immediately, especially after they learned they were both Illyria school teachers. He taught at Windsor Elementary while she taught seventh-grade earth science at Northridge Junior High, and it was almost always the case that Julian's students became her students two years later, so they talked about the kids often. She would tell him how his favorites were doing and he would warn her which ones to look out for.

Over a decade or so, their friendship grew to the point where everyone assumed that Rebecca and Julian were basically a married couple. She was at every dinner party he gave. She knew all his friends. She liked some and didn't like others, especially one named Bruce Bigelow who she had nicknamed, "Bruce The Low," because he was always making nasty little digs at her, as if he was jealous of her friendship with Julian, or perhaps just a misogynist.

In fact, she thought, as the darkened plane continued its trek to Johannesburg, it was at their last Thanksgiving dinner that Bruce had wounded her deeply by something he said. His comment was like the cannon that destabilizes an avalanche, and she hadn't been the same since. They were all sitting around Julian's dinner table, having a raucous good time — and someone had said something rather mean about Julian. The snipe was, "Oh Julian, you're all glands and no heart." Rebecca knew that gay men could be awfully bitchy with each other — it was part of their "game" — but she felt the nasty comment went too far and she had spoken up and said that Julian was the most heart felt and loving person she had ever known. Then Bruce The Low had summarily dismissed her by saying, "Well of course you're going to defend him. You have to. You're his fag hag."

"Bruce, how dare you, I am not!" she shouted, but quickly backed down when others around the table laughed or made ouch faces or added their own loud thoughts. She snuck a look at Julian at the head of the table, but he avoided eye contact with her by taking a sip of his wine, and it was that *avoidance* that disturbed her. He avoided looking at her because he believed those words to be true. She kept trying to tell herself, with all the awful implications of that awful word 'hag', that it wasn't true. But what if it was? What if she was just a fag hag?

It made her want to know then what Julian and she were to each other. It made her want to hear that she wasn't just a "hag." He went to Cleveland to the gay bars to find sex nearly every Saturday night, but this couldn't go on forever, could it? Why didn't he ever want to spend a Saturday night with her, just to go to a movie or to a nice dinner somewhere? Why was their relationship confined to Fridays? Did he really need to go prowling every Saturday?

She wanted to fix this relationship but she didn't know what she was trying to fix. She didn't want to marry him and she wasn't in love with him. "You're his fag hag," Bruce The Low had said, and the meaner of those two words, "hag," kept gnawing at her. What did that word mean anyway? That she was ugly? Or is the hag the woman who always falls in love with gay men because gay men are never going to become sexually intimate? Molly, Joanne and Shannon had gone to become wives and mothers, shuttle drivers, caretakers of fish and hamsters, while she had become the increasingly spinsterish appendage to a gay man — a man who she loved dearly but wasn't "in love" with.

She finally brought it up when they were on the phone one evening.

"Julian," she asked, not waiting for an appropriate moment because she didn't think there could be an appropriate moment, "is that really what I am? Or is that all I am to you, I mean?"

"What? What you are talk about? I'm talking about tattoos."

"I mean what Bruce said, at Thanksgiving."

"What did he say?" (So good at forgetting, she thought.)

"You know... that I'm... that I'm your fag hag." She tripped over the two little words. They barely came out of her mouth.

"No, Rebecca, of course not."

"But what am I then?" she asked, "to you, I mean."

"You're my best friend."

He put it so simply, and it warmed her when she heard him say it. It made everything feel soft again and it temporarily banished her doubt. She decided not to pursue the question to a deeper degree unless it continued to bother her.

Trevor, still sleeping soundly next to her, his head tipped over to the side and almost resting on Rebecca's shoulder, breathed in deeply as if he was short of breath, and then she heard his stomach make a large unhappy growl. She supposed the digestion of that Beef Wellington wasn't going too well and then when she heard the unmistakable sound of flatus escaping his body, she laughed and fanned the air in front of her nose.

We'll always have the fart, she thought.

She loved the human body, in spite of all the trouble it caused.

*

In December of that year, just a few weeks after Bruce's nasty comment, her father called her up one night and complained of pain. When pressed for details, he said it was pain that went from the front to his back, and he added that he couldn't pass his stool. Rebecca's first thought was, "oh my God" because she intuited that it was life threatening. She picked him up and drove him to the Illyria hospital and he was admitted. It was metastatic pancreatic cancer, the kind with a mere four percent survival rate. His pancreas was removed and he began a chemotherapy treatment with a drug called Gemcitabine which gave him headaches and sores in his mouth. His pretentious sister, Victoria, who they deliberately called Vicky to annoy her, began showing up at the house, ostensibly to help. But Willard Over was a proud man and he wanted no one but Rebecca to help him. Rebecca initially agreed that it was better that she care for him so in addition to grading papers and preparing the next day's lesson, she went over to cook for Willard twice a day, and tried to keep the predators and hounds (as Willard now called everyone who wanted to see him) from entering the house.

It was probably more than she could handle alone, and she quickly found herself resenting his somewhat exaggerated helplessness, sometimes even crying about it once she was back in her apartment. She felt like he was purposely acting childish and weak to draw her back into his house. He'd never really accepted it when she moved to her own place so many years ago. But as helpless as he appeared to be around Rebecca, he was still a fiercely opinionated man whenever the subject of his sister came up.

"Father," she asked, as she was setting before him a bowl of Campbell's Chicken Noodle soup, "why don't you let Vicky come over and cook for you one of these days?"

"You know I hate the sight of her," he answered, "and she's a rotten cook."

"It's just canned soup. All you have to do is add water."

"She'd ruin it. Anyway she's just coming around truffling for my money so she can steal it for those five imbecilic birth defects she squeezed out of her."

"I happen to like my cousins."

"You're relentlessly positive daughter. Could I have some toast please?"

She cooked and cleaned for him and tried not to feel resentful. She was frugal and gave herself the excuse that it would be a waste of money to hire a home attendant. The money was practically hers anyway.

(She was so surprised when she had that thought because she never thought herself guilty of rapacity, but money, she discovered, has a strange way of changing positions once mortality makes itself known. She remembered one of those old Illyria tales about a rich eccentric woman who, because she despised her dead husband so much, decreed in her will that her house and money be burned and her body buried in the old Illyria cemetery, as far away from her husband as possible. But the relatives, uninterested in the wishes of a bitter dead woman, sold the house, divvied up the fortune and burned her body instead. And somehow it was all considered legal.)

Money has its own survival instinct, like an animal, and no matter how many times a day her father stared at his portfolio on the computer screen, which seemed to be his only joy these days, Rebecca couldn't help but feel, quite guiltily, that what he was looking at was not his, but hers.

But he did surprisingly well as the weeks passed and the new year arrived. He looked better. He said he felt better. The headaches and nausea and the mouth sores were in retreat. With Rebecca supporting him, he was able to take short walks in his back yard — just to his small bare garden at the edge of the lawn and back. He would breath the cold February air deep into his lungs which he was said was "natural chemotherapy." He said he could feel himself regaining his constitution even though she still had to help him walk from the house to the garden and back.

"Daughter, my body isn't shutting down anymore. I've beaten it." And then he added, "They'll never get me," but like everyone who talks about 'they', he didn't say who they were. Perhaps he meant his sister.

*

A week before Christmas, Rebecca and Julian went shopping at Crocker Park, an Urban Village shopping center with apartments and three storey buildings and streets that go right through the center; all in an attempt to make it feel like a small town. It always made her laugh that a real town like Illyria didn't even have a Starbuck's or any branded business, but the "fake" one was always busy and full of the best stores. The major difference, she thought, besides the parking lots, was that these new small towns didn't have churches.

After Banana Republic, Eddie Bauer and Barnes and Noble, they went to The Cheesecake Factory for a late lunch. Over dessert she told Julian that she needed a vacation and had decided to go to Africa. He answered with an incredulous, "What?" as if it was the craziest idea in the world. "Why would you want to go there?" he asked and she answered, "It's become a dream of mine."

"Since when?"

"Since we watched that movie."

"What movie?"

"*I had a farm in Africa*," she said in her best Dutch accent.

"But that's just a movie."

"I know. But I want to see the real thing."

"Isn't it dangerous?"

"Probably a little. There's always risks."

"And what about the dirt?"

"Dirt has never bothered me."

"What about all the germs?"

"Julian stop it. Children are the germiest creatures alive; how can you worry about germs?"

"Because I use hand sanitizer all day long. I swear some of those kids have the plague, except for Little Miss Myers, of course who has the prettiest little hands with clear painted nails."

Rebecca took another bite of her cheesecake before asking about their favorite fifth grader. "How is the little thing?"

"I've almost given up trying to figure him out. For a boy that effeminate to get along with the others so easily — I don't get it. They never tease him. They let him play with them. But he's got that purse on his wrist and they never ever attack him for it. It's so strange it makes *me* want to tease him."

"But you wouldn't."

"No, of course I wouldn't."

They had gotten off the topic but it was her intention to ask him to join her on this trip so she just came out with it. "So would you like to come with me?" she asked.

"Where?"

"To Africa."

"Oh no," he answered too quickly, "I mean I can't afford anything like that."

"I can pay."

"No I can't let you do that. I wouldn't feel right about it. But what about Orlando? Disney has that safari adventure. I could come down there for a few days and I'm sure it's a lot safer."

"I don't want to do something safe. I want to do something unsafe. "

"Honey, that doesn't make sense."

She thought for a moment about what she really wanted and took the last bite of her cheesecake. "I want to feel like it felt in the movie."

"What feeling was that?"

She wasn't sure. She wanted to call it freedom, but then it might have been romance. Or love. Probably it was none of those. "I don't know exactly," she said, "I want to feel like I'm doing something. That I'm really in the middle of something. Does that make sense?"

"No," he laughed.

She didn't try to explain any further and accepted that Julian was not going to join her on this trip. She resigned herself to taking it alone, which was more than a little scary.

Later, she was in the library looking at a book about the flora and fauna in Botswana and she turned the page and came across a photo of a remarkable bird called the Carmine Bee Eater, a bright crimson bird that flies toward wildfires to catch bugs trying to escape the flames. She was thinking about her fear of traveling alone when she read about the brave little crimson birds that flew toward fire and understood quite suddenly that she had wanted Julian as a crutch, and not as a companion.

"You have to be like that bird Rebecca," she whispered.

Chapter 3

Even though he had felt himself improving in January, Willard Over died in April. His sister immediately became a huge problem for Rebecca, trying to take over the funeral arrangements and behaving as though hers was the more important relationship. The money grubber also wanted to know what provisions had been made for her in her brother's will, but Rebecca refused to tell her.

One reason Willard had hated his sister was because she was constantly putting on airs. Vicky participated in the genealogy craze and felt that being a Mayflower descendant gave bragging rights to the Overtons (somewhere along the way the name was shortened) that more recent immigrants didn't have, more recent being a relative term because Vicky also thought that anyone who arrived after the 1790 census was just "trying to take advantage of America's generosity."

Vicky was so deluded that she once claimed at a Christmas party that Overbrook Road, the fanciest and wealthiest road in Illyria, was named after the Over Family. This had made Willard roar with laughter and say, "Oh Victoria, you're such a horse's ass," in front of all her other guests.

But the real reason she didn't let Vicky have a look at the will (which, if Vicky was the slightest bit imaginative and had snuck into his office, she could have found in the top right drawer of his desk), was not only that Vicky was not named in the will itself, but that her father had attached to it what he had titled, "Very Important Codicil," hand-written, dated only a week prior to his death, and which said, in full legalese jargon, something to the effect that his sister Victoria was entitled to exactly ten pounds of his excrement. The codicil wasn't written by a lawyer and thankfully, neither notarized nor witnessed.

Without consulting her aunt, Rebecca went to see her old high school friend David Miller who had taken over his father's funeral home. She was surprised to learn that David had never married, and they had a nice chat before she told David that she wanted cremation and a simple gold urn. After she made her choice she instantly decided that she would take her father's ashes to Africa and spread them somewhere in the wilderness, far away from the sister and other relations he couldn't stand.

When she told Vicky later that day that she had chosen cremation it was as if she had just damned Willard to hell. They were in her father's kitchen, now her's, standing on either side of the island.

"The Over Family doesn't do cremation!" Vicky loudly insisted.

"Oh please Vicky don't start with the Over Family dos and don'ts again. You know he didn't care about things like that, and neither do I."

"The Over Family doesn't do cremation!" she repeated.

"Why does it matter?"

"He needs a proper burial and a headstone near the family."

"You can bury the ashes if you want and you can have a headstone. I don't mind. I'll give you half the ashes. I'll call

David Miller right now and tell him to put half in an urn for you."

"What's the point of burying ashes?"

"What's the point of burying a body?"

"Oh you are so frustrating Rebecca," she said after slapping the island counter. "You're just like him, you always were. Both of you so thick and pig-headed, and mean-spirited too, I don't mind saying."

"How dare you? Really Vicky how dare you? In my own house..."

"This is his house!"

"It's my house now."

"You don't even act like you're sorry he's dead!" Vicky shouted, and stormed out of the house before Rebecca could answer. "And my name is Victoria and I *want* my *copy* of the *will*," she added just before bursting out the front door.

People who start fights almost always walk away from them, Rebecca thought, rather calmly for how heated the argument was.

Vicky returned later that day of course — her vanity wouldn't allow her to be absent for the guests that wanted to come by and express condolences. Vicky must have eventually resigned herself to the offer of half the ashes because she made no more noise about it, although David Miller had called her to say that her Aunt had phoned demanding an "investigation."

After the funeral home delivered the two urns, however, Rebecca decided to play a trick on her aunt, something, she imagined, would please her father in addition to herself.

She went to the Giant Eagle and asked at the butcher's counter for a large bag of bones — chicken — for soup stock, she said. Once back at her father's house she experimentally put a few of the bones in a cast iron skillet. She put the skillet into the oven and turned the oven to its self cleaning cycle. The self cleaning cycle was about 700 to 800 degrees which she thought was enough to burn the bones, in a controlled way, down to a fine ash. But the smell was so dreadful it almost made her vomit so she abandoned that idea, aired out the kitchen, and went to the giant pet store at the Ridgefield Mall where she bought a five pound bag of finely ground fish tank gravel, with lots of vibrant neon colors.

Back home she took one of the urns into the backyard and dug a small hole in her father's tiny garden where the yellow and white spring crocuses were just starting to poke through the ground. This, she then discovered, was the scariest part of her plan. She crossed herself for absolutely no reason, and carefully removed the top from the urn. The cremains were contained in thick plastic bag which was tightly knotted. After struggling to get it open she carefully poured her father's cremains into the hole. Before covering the ashes with dirt, she took a long look at the "stuff" that had been her father. She was surprised at the appearance, for the ashes were somewhat "chunky" and looked a bit like yellow and off-white sand with tiny bits of black pieces. She assumed the black pieces were the remains of the pine box they used to store him before burning him. The whitish yellow pieces must have been his bones.

Oh, it was so horrible! The only parent she had ever known was this little pyramid of sand now. It was too abstract and the thing they sometimes say at funeral services about "ashes to ashes, dust to dust" really didn't help her because it didn't say anything about what took place between those identical states. What *had* taken place, rather, both good and bad.

Feeling took place, she thought. Ashes — feeling — ashes. Dust — feeling — dust. Generosities. Crimes. We rise up from the dust to feel.

After crying a bit, she gently covered the little pile of his ashes with dirt from the garden and said, "Goodbye Father." Always formal. She thought about how she had walked him back and forth between the house and this garden. It was like she had been walking him to his grave, then bringing him back one last time as a pile of ashes.

Back inside the house, she carefully poured the fish tank gravel into the bag inside the urn and knotted it the way it had been knotted before. She then sealed the top of the urn with an epoxy glue so that Aunt Vicky, if tempted, could not look inside.

At the grave-side service a few days later, Rebecca was standing next to a tree that was just starting to bud, a bit removed from the service itself. Julian didn't like funerals so he hadn't come with her and she stood by herself, separated by a dozen feet from the rest of the mourners. But even at a distance everything about the funeral still pained her. It was such a sad Ohio scene, when they began to sing "Amazing Grace" and could barely be heard above the branches over her head that were swaying in the light wind.

When it came time to place the urn in the ground, Rebecca had to move to the other side of the tree because she didn't know if she wanted to cry or to laugh or to scream. It had been so hard, these last few weeks with her father, and she realized she might have been taking it all out on her aunt. Why, after all, did she really care about her aunt not having the ashes? She took pity on Vicky then, and after the service she tried to hug her, but Vicky just said, "No no none of that," and pushed her away as she turned to leave.

*

In August, when she finally had control of her inheritance and was able to afford the expensive trip to Africa, she visited a travel agent. She told him she wanted to go to Botswana to see the Carmine Bee Eaters. The agent handed her some very colorful brochures about the camps she'd be visiting, as well as some flyers about the rules and regulations — no bright colors or camouflage clothing was allowed, only ten kilograms in one piece of soft luggage. It wasn't until a week before she left and she swallowed her first malaria prevention pill that she felt it deep within that she was actually going to do this. She was going to do it and do it alone.

After swallowing the Lariam, she stared at herself in the mirror, grabbed her pony tail from the force of habit and said, "I still wish you had come, Julian."

*

"I still wish you had come, Julian," she thought again, sitting there in the dark in seat 42D and then wondered if her father's urn was intact in her luggage. They had made her remove the lock in Cleveland and it caused her a bit of anxiety because she wasn't sure if it was legal to travel with someone's ashes.

A hint of gray blue light was starting to seep into the cabin, through window shades that had not been completely shut during the abbreviated evening. She put on the headset to listen to some music which she thought was probably Debussy. Yes it was "Claire de Lune." She looked at the playlist and saw that it was quite extraordinary: "Brahms Intermezzo in A, Opus 118," "Sanguine Fan," by Elgar, "Amour Partes," by Van Wilder, Rossini's "String Sonata No. 1," a Slavonic dance by Dvorak. It suddenly occurred to her how absolutely stunning it all was — that she had flown all the way across the ocean in the belly of a technological sky whale, and was now listening to a recording of Debussy while everything around her came back to life.

Welcome back, she thought.

She had a sense then that the visible world was part of the silent background while the music was on top of it. It was like watching a movie that had music but no other sound effects or dialogue. She stared in awe as the people on the plane began to wake and made treks to the bathrooms in the rear of the plane. She felt humbled and tired. How did they do it? What an amazing thing! They all wake and head for the toilet like animals who urinate in the same spot. Trevor Wardman stirred and yawned next to her but didn't open his eyes. She plugged her nose with her thumb and forefinger, and laughed silently, filled with an unexpected joy about the absurdity of bad breath.

A few window shades were opened by the passengers sitting next to them, and light filled the cabin as if it was pouring into a vacuum. "Claire De Lune" was playing with its floating, trilling, watery sound, and at that moment she suddenly imagined the Carmine Bee Eaters busy along the cliffs near Shakawe.

She saw the fluttering red *oiseaux* against their muddy cliff background: flying, eating, squabbling, feeding — rust colored chicks sitting in the small holes that pockmark the cliffs; staring out at a world that doesn't think about them, waiting patiently for parents with delicious dead crickets. Without realizing it, Rebecca shut her eyes, suddenly overcome with sleep, but she still saw them, those bright birds, with scarlet wings and backs: full of unconscious joy of flight and life. Singing. Calling. Did they know, she wondered, how beautiful they are? She watched as the florid birds suddenly stopped fluttering about and, perched on the edge of their mud nests, with others perched on branches that overhung the dusky water, they turned together as one and stared back at her.

Chapter 4

While waiting in the long line to clear passport control in Johannesburg, Rebecca tried to pick up the signs of a foreign world, but it was antiseptic. She didn't know what she was expecting — she supposed she thought it would be more "African" or something. She sniffed the air a few times to see if she could pick up different scents, but it was air-conditioned and the only thing she could smell was someone's very slight body odor. It didn't bother her. The only smells she couldn't tolerate were cleaning products.

At a picnic one weekend, she had told her old girlfriends that she must have been a bear in a past life, because in addition to her remarkable sense of smell, she had poor eyesight and had always liked "bear food," such as salmon, berries, fruits and nuts. She'd even, to demonstrate, rubbed her back against a tree. While inching along the line, Rebecca smiled to herself thinking about this good memory and the way her three girlfriends had laughed at her antics that day.

They were in their twenties then. Young. Pretty. Fertile.

When it was finally her turn she stepped up to the counter and noticed immediately that the African immigration officer had a vertical scar which bisected his left eyebrow and continued down, crossing over the peak of his very high cheekbone. He had another scar that bisected the right edge of his upper lip. He had obviously been cut deeply — violently. It scared her a little and made her wonder about his past.

She wondered if he had been hurt during the apartheid years, when the country was so sick with violence and hatred. Or was that all forgotten now? She wondered where he lived; if he lived in a township. She wanted to ask him all sorts of questions about his life, and felt slightly embarrassed that she was thinking so much about this man while she hardly ever had similar thoughts about the minority students in her classroom.

She handed him her passport and answered only, "Just tonight. Tomorrow I fly to Botswana," when he asked how long she would be staying. "May I please see your eh-tick-it," he said, and she handed it to him. After peering at it for a moment, he entered some numbers in a computer and finally turned to the first empty page of her passport, slammed it with a stamp and handed it back to Rebecca.

Although there were some bags on the luggage carousel, none of the fifty or so people gathered around it were claiming any of them and no new ones were sliding down the chute. Then Rebecca noticed that a bag on the conveyer above the carousel appeared to be stuck, in one of the turns, blocking everything. No one was doing anything about it.

This was the sort of thing that drove her old friend Joanne totally nuts simply because it delayed her. "Impatient Joanne" would have taken matters into her own hands and jumped right up there to pull the bag out and fix the problem. She remembered the time that she, Joanne, Molly and Shannon had gone to the mall to do some Christmas shopping (before Crocker was built) on some Saturday and on the way back, Route 57 was absolutely packed. Joanne, who was driving, had said, "What are these people doing in my way?" and drove her car up onto the berm and passed all the traffic at a 45 degree angle while the three of them screamed with fear and laughter and all the other drivers beeped their disapproval for not waiting their turn.

But that was a long time ago, before they — the other three — married or went their separate ways. When her father died, they had all called to offer condolences but none suggested getting together for lunch. And she didn't want to ask because she felt, somehow, in the inferior position. She had complained about it to Julian over the phone.

"Oh hon, those class reunion sort of things don't work anyway," he had answered.

"Just for lunch?" she asked, already angry at him but keeping herself calm by shaking her foot. She found that she was increasingly annoyed with Julian, ever since Bruce The Low had called her his fag hag. "We were all very good friends all the way into our late twenties before I met you. I don't see why they can't take a single day off from their damned husbands and kids, or wife in Joanne's case, to have a simple — "

"Listen Rebecca — "

"— No Julian, I'm sorry — not this time."

"Honey! It doesn't matter what they were or they weren't. Don't let it make you bitter. You can't revive an old dead thing. Once it's dead, it's dead. Didn't you read *Frankenstein* in high school?"

"Yes of course — "

"Hey remember that movie? 'What knockers! Oh... zenk you doktor.'"

"I don't know what you're talking about Julian," she said, feeling her impatience rise even further and with her foot shaking ever faster. A movie wasn't what she needed to talk about.

"Gene Wilder. Teri Garr. *Young Frankenstein.* He's talking about the door knockers and says, 'What knockers!' Teri Garr thinks he's admiring her tits and answers, 'Oh... zenk you doktor.'"

"Oh. Yes, that's very funny, Julian," she said, unamused.

"Oh come on Rebecca, you're taking — "

"God damn it Julian, they deserted me! What do you think I'm talking about? I'm not talking about *Frankenstein* or *Dracula* or some movie! They used to love me and now they don't! I'm not sure anyone does!"

There was a horrible stone of silence, while she tried to pull herself together. She wanted to cry, but held it inside until she was able to continue in a calmer tone.

"I'm sorry," she said.

"It's okay," Julian said, but she could tell it wasn't okay.

"They moved on," she continued, but calmly now and explanatory. "They married. They had children. But they didn't include me in — their lives. I love kids. I spend all day with kids, almost every single day of the year. But they didn't even think about including me in their married lives, their families. But I would have included them if I had gotten married. I would have found a way. What did they think? That

I was a lonely spinster? They turned me into the stereotype of an unmarried woman. The cat lady. And I don't even have a cat."

Julian didn't speak for a moment. He may have been thinking about how to phrase his question. "Are you sure that isn't just what you think about yourself?"

"What?"

"You don't know *what* they think about you. They're doing their own thing. They might even think you're better off than they are because you're free. It's probably you who's worried about being single."

"Me?"

"You're the only person who thinks you're a cat lady."

She didn't answer him because he was mostly right. It's what she thought of herself.

And maybe, she thought as she watched other people's luggage pass, the complaints to Julian about her old girlfriends was just a surreptitious way of trying to tell him that she was feeling dissatisfied in their relationship, without saying so directly. It had been her experience that relationship talk was, generally, absolutely terrifying to men. The word alone made them act like they left the car running in the driveway and had to go turn it off.

She probably would have thought about this some more but then Trevor, her foul-breathed neighbor from the plane found her.

"Hi there, still waiting?" he asked.

"Yes, unfortunately," she said.

"I just had a cig in the loo," he said, and Rebecca noticed he was grinning like a bad schoolboy. "I said to myself they can give me a bloody ticket if they want but I haven't had a cig in 24 hours. These damned airports. They force you into withdrawal. It's cruel I tell you. There was no one around anyway."

"So you successfully smoked? Congratulations are in order." As a joke she extended her hand to shake his.

"Thank you very much," he said, shaking hers.

Rebecca could tell that he had also just brushed his teeth after his cigarette and had dabbed some cologne on his neck — because she could smell both tobacco and mint, as well as a pleasant Old Spice kind of scent. She loved the smell of men, even if they were smokers — even if they smoked cigars or pipes. There wasn't, probably, a single man she had ever met that she didn't love the smell of. It had been quite a long time since she had been able to smell a man up close. Years.

It was interesting now how much more attractive Trevor Wardman had suddenly become, now that he had Old Spiced himself up a bit. They chatted until someone finally came and fixed the jam in the conveyer. She caught her bag which, ironically, turned out to be the one causing the jam, and prepared to say goodbye to Trevor and wish him good luck with his television show, but before she was able to leave, Trevor asked her, with a somewhat hesitant voice, if she would like to have dinner.

"I could give you a quick, whirlwind tour of Josie, if you'd like," he said, "show you some of the neighborhoods. Or the mansions if you want. And there's a nice place I think you'd like where they've got great African food and they play jazz all night."

"Mansions?"

"You'll see."

She didn't know what he meant, but immediately perked up at the idea of having a dinner date. It made her feel international, cosmopolitan and exciting. It was a silly feeling but she was enjoying it. Why not? It was the adventure of having, for a short while, a life larger than oneself.

She gave Trevor the name of her hotel, "The Road Lodge," and he laughed, which caused her to pause. He didn't explain why he laughed but promised to call her in a few hours. He'd give her time to have a shower, he said, but they should try to catch what they could during the remaining daylight. He was very proud of himself and she liked the way he looked pleased.

She threw her duffle bag over her shoulder, waved goodbye and left, feeling bouncy about this unexpected date. She followed the other passengers through the declarations area and walked through a set of opaque sliding doors to come out upon a throng of people, who stood in large groups behind metal rails in a kind of gauntlet, and stared at her as she emerged from the confinement of international transit. Most of the faces were black, of course, and she had expected it. But the sudden shock of race made her realize that she was, finally, in the third world.

Chapter 5

Josie

"It's impossible," she said aloud, "that there could be a smaller hotel room anywhere in the world."

There was almost no floor to walk on. The area that was called the "bathroom" wasn't a room at all — it should have been called the "bath corner." It's no wonder Trevor had laughed. This was absolutely terrible. Cheap but terrible.

The shuttle drive to the Road Lodge had been short — it was an airport-convenient hotel only ten minutes away — and she had seen absolutely nothing of Johannesburg. The others on the van had stared straight ahead and looked like zombies between meals. The hotel property was enclosed by a 15 to 20 foot chain link fence with loops of barbed wire at the top. The fellow who had checked her in was a rather short young white man with a very clipped accent in a pressed dark blue uniform and was as efficient, she thought, as a new machine. She had asked him if there was a hotel restaurant to have some lunch. There wasn't and he suggested she use the vending machine which she would have found rude, if he hadn't said it with such perfect politeness.

"No I'm sorry madam, there's nothing but the vending machine, I'm afraid."

"Oh. Well is there anywhere I can *walk to* where I can get some lunch?"

"No madam, I'm sorry, there's nothing, and it's far too dangerous to walk anywhere. The hotel can't be held responsible for your safety if you go outside the perimeter of the premises."

"Oh. Alright then," she had said, more confused than anything. She took her key and left the efficient young man to help the next customer which he was already doing. She found her room, tossed her bag on the bed, then sidled over to the window and opened it to try to clear out the choking smell of the cleaning products. For someone with an acute sense of smell, walking into any place that claimed to be bacteria-free was like walking into room full of mustard gas. The window swung open from the bottom only about 30 degrees, but it would help clear out the cleaning fumes.

She sidled again between the bed and the bureau to a spot where there was a tiny bit of standing room — probably what they called the "dressing room" — to check her bag to make sure her things were okay.

And this was when she discovered that the urn containing her father's ashes was gone.

She started looking through her things. She emptied her purse, knowing it wouldn't fit in there. She removed all the clothes from her bag. She sat on the bed, mentally retraced her path, and tried to remember the last time she saw the urn.

She could remember seeing it sitting on the dining table back home. She had put it there so she wouldn't forget it. And she thought she had checked for it in New York, but she was so flustered by that horrible taxi driver maybe she hadn't. She had to take a yellow taxi from the LaGuardia Airport to the Kennedy Airport, and she was a bit tense because the driver was very gruff, spoke English as a second language and was constantly talking to someone on a speaker that was hanging from his ear. She exited the cab before paying him, which was the wrong thing to do she discovered and the driver had jumped out, inexplicably angry, screaming that she hadn't paid him. She apologized — obviously she wasn't going to run anywhere — and quickly paid, but he wasn't placated. He demanded an extra dollar before opening the trunk, and after she gave him one, he removed her bag and furiously tossed it on the ground, then glared at her as he returned to his car.

And then she had checked it, hadn't she, before checking in?

No she hadn't. She had been worried about missing the flight so she hurried into the building and forgot to check.

She decided to call the front desk. The Efficient Young Man answered.

"I'm sorry," she said, "this is Rebecca Over in room 118. I've lost something very important and I wondered if it might have fallen out of my bag or if someone left it at the front desk. It's a gold colored urn, about ten inches high.

"I'm sorry Madam, nothing's been turned in."

"Are you sure?"

"Yes, quite sure."

"Because it's very important."

"I'm sure it's extremely important Madam but I can assure you there's nothing here and there's nothing been turned in. You said it was gold?"

"Gold colored."

"Was it in your luggage?"

"Yes."

"Then it was probably stolen by one of the airport baggage handlers."

His answer, so matter of fact about the crime, was deflating. She wanted to say "But it wasn't real gold," but realized how useless it would be. There was nothing she could do.

She sat on the bed and wondered if Trevor Wardman was really going to call her. She needed to shower. She crossed the room and stuck her head out of the window to try to breathe some real air, instead of the lung shredding disinfected air of the room. *Look at this*, she thought, *I must look absolutely ridiculous. Anyone who saw me would wonder if I was a lunatic, or think that I was trying to escape some sort of prison.*

After thinking about it a little while, or perhaps because she was able to breath clean fresh air with her head stuck out the window, she realized she wasn't really that distraught over losing her father's ashes. It was just a shock. It had been long enough that she no longer thought of the ashes as being 'him', as when she had that trouble burying the other half in the backyard.

"Enough of this," she said aloud, her head still sticking out of the hotel room window, "It's time to give Julian a call. Let him know I've arrived."

She calculated that it was around 1 p.m. back in Ohio, so she called his cell phone.

"Hellooo? Rebecca? It says 'international call' so I hope that's you, sweetie?"

"Julian? Can you hear me?"

"I can hear you just fine Rebecca. Don't shout. Where are you?"

"The flight was very long and I didn't sleep at all. How are you?"

"I'm the same as I was when I dropped you off at the airport yesterday. Can you hear me okay?"

"Oh wonderful. It's warm and the days appear to be very long. It's only just now starting to get dark."

"Rebecca! Can you hear me?"

"Yes, I can hear you just fine. Listen, Julian something's happened."

"What was that? Hang on. I'm going under a bridge. Might fade... but... anyway... Rebecca? Hello? What did you say?"

"I have bad news!" she shouted.

"What? Are you okay? You're not hurt, are you? Are you in the hospital? What happened?"

"I'm fine Julian, I just... I lost the ashes."

"Oh my God. You lost his ashes? How?"

"I don't know. I think someone stole them, or stole the urn."

"What are you going to do?"

"Well I'll ask if I can check the shuttle bus but that's about all I can do. The hotel's in the middle of nowhere and they said it's dangerous to walk anywhere."

"How can it be dangerous if it's in the middle of nowhere?"

"That's just what they said."

"Well I'm sorry Rebecca. I know you really wanted to do that for him."

"Thanks Julian, but why are *you* sorry?"

She could hear Julian sigh at the other end, annoyed by her stupid question. "Stop. Forget it. That was just a dumb question. Thank you Julian. That's all I meant to say. But listen I'd better go. I'm sure this is costing ten dollars a minute. I just wanted to let you know I made it."

"Well you be careful, okay sweetie?"

"I will."

"And have a good time. And don't worry about your father's ashes, he won't know and he won't care and I'm sure he'd forgive you anyway. Anyway, I can't wait to see the pictures. So take lots. If they have Email there try to send some."

"I will."

"Miss you already," he said.

"Me too."

She felt reassured after speaking with Julian. The hotel phone rang as soon as she had replaced the receiver and she answered it. It was Trevor, asking if she was ready for her tour.

"As ready as I'll ever be," she said, her stomach suddenly turning over in knots.

*

Trevor took her first, while there was still some daylight, to a wealthy section of Johannesburg which he referred to as the mansions. They were enormous homes built on huge pieces of land and every single home was behind very tall white concrete walls with layers of barbed and electrified wire at the top, making it hard to see anything but the upper floors and roofs. Most had a staffed guard's station at the driveway entrance. Though there were lots of light purple flowering Jacaranda trees which were beautiful to look at, the appearance of the stark white concrete walls on either side of the road, stretching off to the distant ends, gave her a feeling she couldn't identify — something to do with a slightly guilty feeling she had that she was spying on the rich. Black men and women in blue or green or pink uniforms walked between the road and the walls. They seemed very distinctively on the "outside." She wondered if this was her first visible encounter with apartheid. But she didn't know.

"Why are all the homes behind walls?" she asked.

"That's the way we do it here. The first time I saw one of your American suburbs I couldn't understand it. All those exposed homes the whole world can see? Nothing protected? This is a very dangerous country. The richest people in Africa live in this neighborhood and they have to protect themselves. It's no different than Hollywood. Those houses are protected and hidden from prying eyes too."

"But we're the ones with prying eyes, aren't we?" she asked, but Trevor made no reply, a silence which she took to be an annoyed one. Whether he was annoyed or not, she was right. They were the ones looking over the walls.

The restaurant he took her to was called Moyo which, according to the menu, was the Swahili word for "soul." He told her they were in the Melrose Arch section of Johannesburg, but that had no meaning for her. The restaurant was five levels joined together by a huge granite staircase and steel and copper plated bridges. What sounded like a type of African jazz music played throughout. There was a giant Moroccan tent that you went through to get into the 'Blue Room'. It was really quite magnificent, she thought, and the menu was filled with items she couldn't pronounce like Mpumalanga and Umfino which, the description stated, was "grilled gebna." She laughed because even with a translation she still didn't know what it was. She settled on a Hermanus Shrimp Tian to start, which was a mix of avocado, shrimp, tomato and basil, and Mascarpone cheese. For dinner, turning down Trevor's first suggestion to order the Ostrich, she selected Seven Steps Kingklip, a fish cooked with traditional South African Cape Malay spices.

"We don't have anything like this at home," she said to Trevor.

"It's all McDonald's in America isn't it?"

"It's not all McDonald's," she said, "but there's almost no restaurant in Illyria that isn't part of a large chain. But Illyria's a very poor town and getting poorer by the year. The corporate restaurant is probably the only option for a town like ours."

"Accggh," he said, and she noted the throaty way he said 'acch.' "People are lazy. They want everything done for them. All the bloody Afs in this country want free water, free electricity, free homes. They think Whitey got it for free all those years, so why shouldn't they? It's no use telling them we pay for our services and always have. They don't believe us."

"Can they afford to pay?"

"Of course they can. But the Afs are lazy."

The first time he used the term 'Af', she thought she might be offended. The second time, she was.

"I assume when you say 'Af' you mean 'African'?"

"Yes, obviously," he said with a slight tone of annoyance.

"May I ask, Trevor, are you not an Af also?"

He laughed. "No I'm a white. 'Af' is what whites say instead of 'kafir' since that word is illegal now. People say "K" to get around it."

His racism and general manner turned her against him and she had zero interest in talking with him any longer. After dinner she made the excuse that she had to get up before dawn to catch the plane to Botswana, which was the truth anyway, and asked Trevor if they could skip desert and return to her hotel.

On the drive back, she realized she hadn't really "seen" Johannesburg the way she had expected to see it, and she said to Trevor, "It's hard to know what to say about Johannesburg. Or Josie as you call it. There are a lot of roads and highways, but it's hard to see anything."

"Accgggh. Traffic is horrible here."

"It doesn't seem like there's a center."

"No you don't want to go to the city. Too dangerous. If you want to go to the city you have to have one of those cars that shoot flames from the side."

"Excuse me?"

"I'm not joking. Car-jacking is one of the worst problems here. That and rape and they usually go together. Some cars come now with a safety feature in the trunk that lets you lock all the doors of the car and open the trunk, in case you're forced into it. That way the car jackers can't escape."

"Are you serious?"

"That's what they do, these bloody K's. They steal your car with you in it, and then take you somewhere to rape the living daylights out of you. It's terrible."

"But where were we for dinner? That seemed quite safe."

"That's a suburb."

"I see," she said. "In America they called it the white flight. Probably in twenty or thirty years you'll all be moving back to the city."

"I doubt it," he said. "You'll never get whites and blacks to mix, except for the namby ones that feel sorry for everyone."

She hated this man.

After they had been let through the hotel's gate, Trevor pulled up to the drop off location and looked over at Rebecca with an expectant smile. He apparently thought she was going to invite him up. She looked at him and said, "Thank you Trevor. I had a very nice time. Thank you for showing me Johannesburg." She opened the door.

"Well hold on," he said, "Can I give you my phone number, for when you come back through again? I'd love to take you out again if you have the time."

"Sure," she said, and waited while he fished a card from his wallet.

Back in her room she looked at his card, thought "horrible racist," and tossed the card in the trash can. She turned on the television, stretched across her bed and watched a talk show that was being conducted in Afrikaans. It was a thick and throaty language with words that sounded difficult to pronounce — almost sounded as though they could strangle the speaker. But it sounded, she thought, like it might be a wonderful language for cursing or getting angry. It had that nice Germanic core. It was good for pirates too, society's bachelors, like Julian the butt pirate, as they roam the seas and shout, "Hip hip, hooray," for killing the crew and burning the ships of enemies, until the peg-leggedy captain, whilst lost in the doldrums for days upon days, praying for some wind and movement, thinks finally of the many ways to attack and rape a lower ranked seaman. Pitiless seamen. Always raping. Always raping the weaker ones. Sexual with dirty fingers. Bastards. Bastards if not aborted. Untie the semen knot, for shocked they'd be if blue they knew. If anyone knew, would they forgives us? Spectacles testicles. And all those friends of

Jules's who izzes and laugh or tatter and liff or titter and titter. Hmmm? What?

She jerked suddenly awake. Confused and very dazed, like she'd been knocked on the head, Rebecca stared at the television at some people who talked in a tangled language.

She was alert enough to arrange a wake up call, then she quickly turned off the television and the lights, stripped down to nothing as she liked to sleep nude and slid under the stiff sheets of the bed. In spite of the chemical odor in the room, which wasn't nearly as bad now that it had been aired all evening, the bed was unbelievably comfortable, and she felt every single muscle in her body relax and sink deeper into the mattress as if each strand of her body was melting, coming lose. Though she wasn't directly thinking about it, something made her think, while disappearing into the geographically unlimited haze of hypnagogic thought, that the reason she didn't care about losing her father's ashes was because she just didn't want her Aunt Vicky to have them, that's all it was, except, she thought, as she disappeared further into unguarded unconsciousness, she still felt she would rather have not had the abortions, and maybe that was why she had wanted to spread the ashes under a tree, because of the abortions.

But there was nothing she could do about that, anyway, and it was a long time ago, so without thinking anything more, she fell asleep, deeply and completely, for the first time since leaving America.

Chapter 6

Duba

Her jet lag and internal alarm woke her in time for her to shower, re-pack her suitcase, rush down to the lobby for a badly needed continental breakfast, and make it back to the airport in time to leave South Africa and enter Botswana's Okavango Delta, via Gaborone and Maun. On the first leg to Gaborone, she realized that she had been in such a rush that she had forgotten to ask the shuttle driver if he had found the urn. She knew he hadn't and she tried not to worry herself over it — although it gave her, the couple of times she let herself think about it, a vague feeling of discomfort which was not a feeling she wanted to have as she began this trip.

The jet, a Boeing 727 operated by Air Botswana, landed in Gaborone and parked on the tarmac near two straight walkways that were separate by about ten feet: one that led into the international side of the small airport and one that went from local side, back to the plane. The plane would remain there until all its passengers had shuffled through and received their appropriate stamps and permissions. The landscape here was as flat as it was in Ohio, but much drier and dustier. The grass on either side of the sidewalk was green but stubbly.

On the way up the first sidewalk, Rebecca noticed some ants scrambling all over the pavement, and she pulled out her magnifying glass to have a closer look. The sidewalk was narrow and a somewhat tubby man walking behind her made an impatient scowl as he stepped onto the ragged grass to get around her. Just as he did, the strap on one of his bags came loose and he dropped it.

"Mon Dieu," he muttered and before bending down to pick up his bag, turned and gave Rebecca a half stare which she caught and took to mean that it was her fault his bag broke. She knew it wasn't her fault but didn't blame him for his impatience. *Traveling this far is stressful*, she thought as she waited for him to recover and continue up to the airport. In the line to have her passport stamped the little man was joined by a woman, taller than he, and two children — she presumed his wife and kids. His wife, she thought, was beautiful in a way that didn't go with him. She was serene and he wasn't. They looked like a mismatched couple.

Their next airport stop was in the town of Maun and was the most unusual place she had yet seen, at least what she could see of it from the air as they came in for the landing. It was the most African place she had been so far, if that was an acceptable way to describe it. Some of the houses were small and round and brownish — like dried clay — with thatched, pointed roofs. Others were small square houses which looked to be made of cement blocks. Each home, whether square or round, had a fence of wood surrounding it, but at awkward unmeasured angles, making everything look like a patchwork of different trapezoids and quadrilaterals. Almost every piece of property was devoid of grass — just pounded dirt — with perhaps a few bushes and a leafy green tree or two. She noticed that the tiny Maun airport was located almost in the exact center of the village.

After she disembarked she entered the Maun airport and was surprised because she heard someone call her name.

"Rebecca Over?" A thin, tall white woman with short black hair was walking over to her as if they had business to discuss.

"Yes that's me. How did you know?"

"Lucky guess I guess. We're just waiting for the DeKoning Family and I'll pass you off to Jordan who's going to handle your luggage and take you through security." She was constantly looking at a clipboard in one hand and at a walkie talkie in her other. She spoke into it, "Jordan? Jordan Jordan Jordan," but there was no answer and she said to Rebecca, "acch," as if Rebecca would understood her frustration.

"Are you from the travel agency?" Rebecca asked.

"Nope. Nope. I'm from the charter company. The planes."

"Well I was wondering if we would had time to see a bit of Maun?"

"No unfortunately you've got to fly right out again. The schedule's a bit tight and Air Botch-it was late again. Anyway Maun's nothing but a donkey town. Nothing interesting to see here." She spoke into her walkie talkie again, "Jordan, Jordan, Jordan," to no avail, and then said to Rebecca, "and I bet these are the Belgians."

The DeKoning Family turned out to be the same family Rebecca had noticed in Gaborone. The Botswanan porter that the woman had been paging showed up at the same time. They identified their luggage which Jordan collected and carried without a cart — all five pieces — which Rebecca thought was astounding. As Rebecca felt herself herded along, the American representative explained that they were all going to the same camp. They were rushed through another metal detector, another luggage scanner and then she was suddenly facing a woman who asked for her passport and to "please state how many weapons" she was carrying.

"What?" Rebecca said, instantly frightened.

"Are you hunting?" the woman asked.

"Oh. No. No. Never. None," she said.

She looked around but the American representative had already vanished and it was now Jordan's turn to rush them along. She hated this feeling of being maneuvered or pushed along, but she knew this was part of the process of being a tourist. Still it would have been nice to see Maun, this "donkey town," she thought.

Jordan took them back out to the tarmac where what looked like about fifty small planes were parked at evenly spaced intervals. They walked over to a six seat Cessna. The pilot, who had very big ears, a nice Australian accent and gorgeous teeth, introduced himself as Conrad and after getting the bags packed and the DeKoning family seated in the rear seats he told Rebecca to climb through his door and sit in the co-pilot's seat.

"But I can't fly a plane," she objected.

"It's just for balance," he said, smiling, "but if anything happens to me, you'll have to land the plane. Just grab the handles, look for an open strip of grass and try not to hit any elephants, alright love?"

She knew he was joking but nevertheless climbed into the co-pilot's seat with a dire feeling as Conrad gave them a few safety instructions about the seat belts and air sickness bags. Looking behind her, Rebecca could see the impatience of Mr. DeKoning. He had interlaced his fingers and was actually twiddling his thumbs. Thumb chasing thumb. She smiled at him when he noticed her looking at him but he just looked away, as though it was an irritation to be seen.

"Have you been to Botswana before?" she asked him, while Conrad strapped himself into the pilot's seat and prepared the plane. She felt very excited and anxious and wanted to talk.

"Yes many times," he answered without looking at her, and volunteered nothing more, so Rebecca faced forward and left him alone.

She held her breath as the plane took off because the feeling in the small plane was significantly different to the feeling on the jet and it made her much more nervous, being able to see so much of the sky and the ground beneath. But by the same token she finally had a view of what the world looked like for soaring birds, and what she saw was what looked like, but she knew couldn't possibly be, the entire country of Botswana. The view went off so far into the distance it was hard to tell whether or not it disappeared or ended simply because of the limitations of the human eye. The world seemed to fade into the horizon and she had a momentary sense of everything, including time, blending together somewhere beyond what she could see.

She turned around to look at the Belgian family and saw that the father had fallen asleep, his mouth was open and as slack as a rubber band. His wife and children were, like her, staring down at the landscape beneath the plane. They flew over a fence that went off in a straight line as far as they could see which Conrad shouted to her was called the Buffalo Fence. It kept the humans and their livestock on one side and the wild animals on the other.

"Originally it was to keep the wild animals out of the human area, but now it's to keep the humans out of the wild side, otherwise they'd come up here with their cattle and goats and eat the lot."

The contrast was shocking, for on the southern side of the fence — the human side — the land was mostly dirt, albeit with plenty of healthy green trees, but once over into the animal side the land turned thick with tall green grasses and bushes, and the water everywhere was a deep cobalt blue. Nothing on this northern side was grazed by the roaming cattle or goats, and the entire sun-drenched vista, as far as she could see, was dappled with tiny islands of palms or other trees she couldn't identify. Surrounding every island, in patterns that resembled the dendrites that surround a neuron, were animal tracks that had been randomly pounded through the recently flooded grass. The French horns from the *Out of Africa* soundtrack started replaying in her mind, and chills raced up her arms to the back of her neck.

This was the most beautiful thing she had ever seen. She was aware that some sort of emotion was starting to well inside her, just behind her throat.

"All the islands are made by termites," Conrad shouted to her.

"Termites?"

"Yes. The termites eat all the wood and build huge termite mounds. The mounds are higher than the flood so eventually plants and trees take root and survive and that's how all these little islands are formed. They grow."

"How deep is the water?"

"Maybe up to your knees. Not deep at all. In a month it'll all be gone."

And then, as she stared at the scene and took it in with her eyes like a feast, and without quite realizing it at first, because it took her a moment to understand what she was looking at, she spotted her first large wild animal.

"What is that? What? An elephant! I see an elephant!" she shouted, "Conrad I can see an elephant!"

Conrad tilted the plane so he could look out Rebecca's window. "Yes you're right Rebecca, there it is, isn't it?" He straightened the plane again. "I'd take us down for a look-see but we're not allowed to frighten them. Aww' but it's great fun to chase a herd of impala or buffalo. I don't think it really scares them. They just run 'cause all the others run."

She had her hand on her heart and she thought for a minute that it was going to break. From the air the elephant was just a small speck of dark grey, but she was able to see it moving slowly through the shallow blue green water. There were ripples around its legs. It was really alive — living its life in the wild — walking somewhere — and it was, she thought, the most extraordinary thing she had ever seen. She faced forward to think about this moment and was so overwhelmed and surprised at what she was feeling that she had to cover her mouth with both her hands and began to cry.

"Are you alright Rebecca?" Conrad asked.

"I'm just... yes." She smiled to reassure him and fanned her face. "I didn't expect," she said, but left the sentence unfinished and returned her gaze to looking for more animals while grabbing hold of her ponytail. She felt an alteration inside and it was unexpectedly painful but okay. It was as though a piece of plaque had just been removed from the surface of her heart. She didn't know why it felt this way. Of course she'd hardly ever taken a vacation before.

She sensed eyes on her neck and turned to see the Belgian father staring at her with what she thought was a look of disgust. He probably didn't like Americans. That was certainly the case in many areas of the world if the news was accurate. Maybe she had woken him when she screamed with such silly exuberance. "Sorry," she said, and smiled once again. But he just folded his arms across his belly, leaned his head against the window and closed his eyes to go back to sleep. She thought of a momentarily annoyed cat. She dried her eyes. The strange man had, oddly, brought her back to her senses.

After the Cessna landed on a small strip of dirt — how had Conrad had been able to find it in that vast wilderness she couldn't guess — they were met by the camp's manager, Felix, a bright blonde man in his thirties who looked just as she expected an African Safari camp manager would look: deeply tanned, wearing a hat and khakis, with strong muscular legs that were barely contained by his tight shorts. Felix drove them into the camp and a petite Botswanan woman who he introduced as Peaceful, greeted them with orange juice in fluted glasses.

"Oh how glamorous," Rebecca said as she accepted hers, "to be greeted with orange juice in the middle of Africa."

"Mimosas actually," Felix said. "Is this your first time to the Delta?"

"Guilty as charged," Rebecca said, feeling herself blush. To cover her blush she asked the woman, "Can you tell me your name again?"

"Peaceful," she said.

"I thought that's what you said. What a pretty name you have."

"Oh you'll meet all sorts of Botswanans with funny names in English," Felix said, and then rattled off a few, "Cheerful. Ugly. Stinky. Beautiful. It's a third world thing to name your child after an adjective."

She stopped herself from pointing out that Felix meant "lucky" in Latin. She thought it was strange that he talked about the Botswanans so bluntly, but Peaceful didn't seem the slightest bit concerned.

Rebecca and the Belgian family enjoyed their mimosas for a minute more and then they were shown to their "tents," which were nothing like the traditional tents one thinks of in talks of camping, but huge rooms with hardwood furniture, large comfortable beds, running water, basins and showers.

"This is nicer than my apartment," she said to the young Botswanan man who had carried her bag and shown her to the tent.

"Eh..." he said, and she thought she heard him add something like the word "mud" without the "d." "Muh," or something like that.

"It's just beyond anything I imagined."

"Eh... muh."

"I couldn't be happier."

"Come to thee frrrrrront when you are rrrready," he said and left.

She said to herself while she unpacked her things, "Oh Julian you don't know what you're missing. You should have accepted my offer and joined me."

She held the blouse she was unpacking to her heart and looked around the room again. The tent was outfitted with a whicker chair, a writing desk, and it had its own balcony. There were white curtains covering all the canvas panels and there was a very soft breeze coming in the room. She was tempted to lie down for a bit, not only because she was quite tired, but because it was so beautiful she wanted to fully appreciate it, or take it in somehow. But she didn't want to risk falling asleep and missing her first activity, so she decided to hang up her clothes and have a quick shower in time to go to the lounge up front where the guests would be gathering to have tea before going on their early evening drive.

The lounge at Duba was open on two sides and fitted with two huge couches and chairs, along with a bar toward the enclosed rear part of the room. The dining room was also open-aired so from almost everywhere in the camp the African landscape was the dominant feature of one's vision. Unlike the airport in Johannesburg, you couldn't *not* feel like it was Africa. The landscape was your wall. She sat on one of the couches and stared out at it, still not quite believing it was all real and that she had come to the other side of the planet and was sitting there looking at it.

"How are you getting along?" Felix asked when he stepped into the lounge.

"I couldn't be happier. This is incredible."

"Wonderful. Always glad to hear that. We'll have tea in a bit and meet the other guests — three Americans like you — and then we'll take our first drive. The game's a bit scarce out there but I'm sure we'll see a few good things."

"Is something wrong?"

"No, no. It's just the wet season now and the animals are more spread out and harder to spot. There's a lot more to eat. In the summer it's so dry they all have to come closer — for the water holes."

"Oh."

"Shoo it gets dry here." Felix made a flicking motion with his fingers when he said that funny word. "You wouldn't recognize it Rebecca. Everything looks as dead as can be. And if the wild fires come through. Shoo. But now it's lovely and green. I'm sure we'll see something. This area has more lions than any other camp so we'll likely come across a pride. I'll leave you to it then. Be back in a bit."

A Botswanan man dressed in an official green shirt and khaki pants that were heavily frayed at the cuff and the back pockets came into the lounge and he introduced himself as Lesh. When he extended his right hand to shake hers, he used his left hand to touch the nook of his right elbow which seemed like one of those gestures of respect that was meant to show you had nothing in your other hand. Lesh said he would be her guide and asked Rebecca what she would like for her sunset drink: Coke, orange squash, Fanta, gin and tonic, tea.

"Gin and tonic, isn't that the African drink?"

"Okaaaay," he said politely, smiling and clearly not actually hearing her question.

When the Belgian family came into the lounge, Rebecca was steeping some tea, and was amused when the father asked Lesh, who was still standing behind the bar preparing drinks for the drive, for "a lot of sparkling water and a piece of dark chocolate — no milk."

Lesh looked around, smiling and hopelessly puzzled over the "no milk" demand as the father went to have a seat on the couch and quickly busied himself reading an old tattered magazine. Rebecca decided to introduce herself and walked over to where he was sitting.

"Excuse me, I don't think we've formally met. I'm Rebecca Over."

"Yes?" he said, looking puzzled.

"I'm Rebecca Over."

"And?"

His wife intervened by quickly coming over to the couch with her arm extended, saying in very good English accent, "I'm Elizabeth DeKoning and this is my husband Marcel."

The children, two little dark haired imps, came over and were introduced as Anton and Griet and although they didn't speak English one could sense they, like Marcel's wife, were pleasant and kind. The children, in particular, made her feel doubly good because as Elizabeth and Rebecca sat and chatted she would occasionally look at the children to see if they had begun to play on their own. But every time she looked they would instantly smile at her, as if they had been waiting for another chance to make her feel welcome. They had an eagerness she wished her 7th grade school children had.

Marcel sat with them off to the side and appeared to half listen while he leafed through some of the old battered magazines. Periodically he scoffed or harrumphed at some of the things Rebecca said about her life back home, or seemed to. She wasn't sure. He might have been scoffing at the magazine.

The other guests arrived in due course — three men from Michigan — and after tea and introductions she, the

DeKonings and the three men whose names she had already forgotten, gathered up their cameras and binoculars, hats and birding books, and were shown to their vehicle by Lesh. The passenger seats of the modified Land Rover were a set of three risers, each row higher than the next, and Marcel had already climbed to the top row of the vehicle, apparently wanting the highest seat. Rebecca sat directly behind Lesh on the lowest level. She wanted to able to hear what he had to say.

Felix was correct that the animals were scarce, but it was stunning, even without animals. The land nearer to the water looked as if newly painted out of nothing, with vast empty areas of light green covered with tiny yellow wildflowers looking as though they'd been applied with a stippling brush. The scent of the air was surprisingly moist and pleasant, and there were magnificently colored birds which Lesh stopped and pointed out and allowed everyone to check off of the lists they were provided.

They spotted the Yellow Billed Hornbill, some Redbilled Quelea, different kinds of bright yellow weaver birds and their round elaborate nests hanging from trees in clustered bunches. They saw a column of vultures rising slowly into the stratosphere on what Lesh said was an updraft of heat which is why they didn't have to flap their wings but just slowly circled, effortlessly rising higher and higher. They came across Botswana's national bird, the Lilac Breasted Roller sitting on the top of a dead six foot termite mound, just staring back at them. And there were many large ground birds like the extremely noisy Hadeda Ibis, the Hamerkop and the weird looking Maribou Stork which someone said looked like a hunchbacked butler.

When they did get to see large animals like buffalo and impala they were very far away and Lesh said not to waste pictures on them. He said they were "ugly," which made Rebecca respond, "Oh really," but because of his smile she knew he was joking. But it was disappointing that Lesh wouldn't take them closer and seemed not to care about them.

After an hour it appeared their first drive was going to be a failure, other than seeing a lot of birds and a few larger animals off in the distance. In all her preparatory reading she had come to expect it. "Nature's not a zoo," one of the magazines had warned. But she had hoped that on her first game drive the animals would not be as scarce as this.

Just then, Lesh stopped the vehicle and said, "Ohhhh. O-kaaaay." He took out his binoculars and looked off in the distance.

Rebecca's pulse quickened and she looked in same the direction but saw nothing but a small stand of green trees and tall shrubs. He turned around, pointed to the same grove of trees she was looking at and said very quietly to the group, "Do you see?"

"I can't see anything," Rebecca whispered, looking through her binoculars. Nobody else seemed to be able to see either. But with the exception of Marcel who was still napping in the back, they continued to scan the area with their binoculars. And then Rebecca saw what Lesh was pointing at. It was an elephant.

"We will get closer," Lesh said, "she is giving both."

"Both?"

"Birth," Marcel said, suddenly rousing from his torpor and standing to unpack his camera and make preparations while simultaneously holding onto the bar for balance. Rebecca turned around because the energy in this little man was suddenly quite dynamic and a bit contagious. "This will be absolutely extraordinary," he said, "you people are all very, very lucky. You have no idea. Some people come their whole lives to see something like this and never do."

It was the first time Marcel had shown any interest in anything at all and she noted he said "you people" not "we." She was surprised to see him take out a camera that was larger than any she had ever seen. It was bigger than his head.

"Are you a professional photographer Marcel?"

"Yes of course I am," he said petulantly, as he connected some gadget to another gadget. Lesh was driving slowly and he brought the vehicle to a stop at a further distance than he normally would, he said, because this was a very vulnerable time. "She is always surprised," he said in a low voice.

"What do you mean?" Rebecca asked, leaning forward and using the same quiet voice.

"She is always surprised," Lesh repeated.

"Surprised?"

"She does not know what is happening."

"But how do you know she's giving birth?" Rebecca asked.

"You see how she is walking? Back and forth and side to side, like she is a disturbed. She is in labor and she doesn't know what it is. She has been getting fat for two years," he held up two rough fingers for emphasis, "and now something is happening. She maybe think she is dying. But she is going to find out." And he laughed.

"I can't see," Rebecca complained, fumbling with her binoculars.

"Look at the area around her lower... ehhhh... belly."

When she managed to re-focus on the abdomen she saw two small legs sticking straight out of the mother, much lower on the body than she expected, toward the ground, and she abruptly paled and almost recoiled.

"The back legs come first, and then the frrrront and the head," Lesh said. "Not the same as people."

"How long will it take?" one of the American men asked.

"I don't know. Once the legs come out it is usually soon."

Rebecca was shocked by the sight of those tiny but huge back legs sticking out of the elephant cow, but she didn't know why. It gave her a queasy feeling, and felt almost, like a surreal painting; something you expect to see but aren't quite sure what you're looking at when you see it. It was as if it was impossible.

Marcel's camera was snapping away like mad. Twick twick twick twick. "We must get closer Lesh," he demanded. She turned around to frown because Marcel wasn't using a quiet voice, but to Rebecca's surprise, Lesh started the vehicle as commanded and moved closer. Perhaps he had been told that this man was a professional photographer and was to do what he said.

When they were about two hundred feet from the elephant — the distance you would be at a zoo — Rebecca no longer needed her binoculars to watch the ordeal. The mother elephant paced forward and backward, then side to side, and she looked terribly distraught. She looked, Rebecca thought, as if she was crying for help. Several times she lifted one of her giant rear legs in the air, as if trying to make more room to push it out. At another point she actually got down on her front knees and kept her rump in the air, but then she quickly stood again and continued the side to side/backward and forward tormented motion.

"Is she in pain?" Rebecca asked.

"Yes," Lesh answered, "the baby is 250 pounds and he is ready to walk and eat."

She went faint again, because she thought of her own weight of 125. After five more minutes, while Rebecca held onto her ponytail and clenched her pelvic muscles, the 250 pound baby elephant slipped out and landed on the ground in a huge rush of blood and amniotic fluid. It was like a giant tank emptying out.

The mother elephant then backed away with extreme care; Rebecca was astonished at how gently the elephant was able to walk. She backed away to see what had just come out and it was exactly as Lesh had said. She was startled and almost jumped. Her giant ears flipped forward defensively and she quickly backed away from the inert baby as if it was dangerous.

Then, so carefully it was almost timid, she stretched out her truck from the farthest distance possible to have a sniff.

But it, the baby, had not moved. Oh God, she hoped it wasn't dead.

"Is it alive?" Rebecca whispered. Marcel's whirring camera was really starting to irritate her. Twick. Twick. Twick. It was an unnatural sound. Everyone else was taking pictures but not one after the other like a machine gun.

Lesh was peering through his binoculars at the baby on the ground. "Is it alive?" she asked again, in a whisper. "He hasn't moved yet."

"Yes," Lesh said, "he is alive. Now we will watch as he tries to walk and take his first drink from da' titty."

The elephant baby finally moved and struggled to stand up for the first time. It had a hard time doing so, but once it was finally up on all fours, it took its first wobbly steps toward the mother. He was still covered in blood and what might have been the caul or white mucous. And although it was clear that the mother had instantly accepted the baby into her care, there was nothing she could do to help the baby find the teat. It had to learn on its own. And Rebecca couldn't tell where the teats actually were, because she was thinking that it was more like a cow or a goat, and that they should be toward the back between the rear legs. But the elephants' breasts are near the front armpits, which she could see when Lesh pointed them out. They looked, in fact, very human — the way it would look if a naked woman was on all fours, her breasts hanging down.

It was frightening, watching this first lesson, because it took such a long time for the baby to find the breast that it seemed like it was never going to happen. Her scientific mind knew that the baby wasn't going to die instantaneously if he didn't find the breast within three minutes. Nature wasn't so stupid as to waste two years on a three minute race for food, but emotionally she was terrified. For ten minutes, she found herself saying, "come on, come on," and getting frustrated when the baby would press its mouth against the side of his huge mother. She muttered things like, "Not there," or "No, toward the front little elephant." Lesh just laughed at her and said, "Don't worry Miss R-r-r-rebecca, he will find it. He always find it."

"He has to," she added.

The baby elephant had no control over its trunk, which hung from its head like a strange limp appendage, and very little control over its wobbling legs. It plopped itself down for a minute, as if petulant and too used to the rosy life of the womb, but the mother prodded it repeatedly with her trunk until it stood again, and he started searching for the teat again. After what seemed like an eternity, and many more attempts at suckling at the side of her body or toward the rear from where he had just emerged, he poked his lips in the right place and found it. And then he knew. An extraordinary change came over the baby elephant which was visible on his skin, like a patina of streaked silver, and over the mother's face too, once he had found it. They looked...as though everything was accomplished.

Lesh said, "Ahhh. You see. Once a man knows where da titty is, he never forget," and he laughed along with everyone else. While the elephant baby suckled, his little trunk fell off to the side, still useless. The mother elephant waited, stood like a gray statue, while the baby took his first drink, but she soon began to move in a particular direction, and the baby followed alongside, his legs not as wobbly. It was as if she knew where to go, and he, her new two year old newborn, knew that he was supposed to follow her.

"She will take him back and introduce him to the rest of the family now," Lesh said, and they watched quietly as the mother and her baby turned away from them, pushed through some tall green bushes and disappeared.

There was something about the way these two enormous creatures disappeared so quickly that made Rebecca gasp. She didn't know why it shocked her, or why it should, but it was as if the world had shown her something and then suddenly turned off the picture. She knew it was absurd but still, she had the strange and somewhat unsettled feeling she was being taught, and that there was something else taking place here.

Chapter 7

As they prepared to drive off in search of a picturesque spot for their sundown tea where Marcel would finally get to eat a piece of dark chocolate, Rebecca leaned forward and asked Lesh, "What do you think the baby thinks about all of this?"

"The baby?" he asked.

"Yes," she said, "It must be such a shock for a creature like that to come into the world. Conscious and ready to walk. Not to mention the shock of the poor mother suddenly being 250 pounds lighter. In the womb he probably thought he was a spirit. But suddenly he discovers he's an animal with a body that moves through the world."

Lesh smiled at her, because she hadn't asked a question and because he probably didn't understand what she was talking about, and he answered, "Ohhh ohh-kay," in his long slow friendly way, while Rebecca, feeling a bit conflicted and weirdly deflated, leaned back in her seat and thought about what she had just watched. Marcel was speaking French in the rear of the rover, thinking that Rebecca didn't understand French. "*Que dit-elle maitenant?*" His wife replied in English, "shut up," which gave Rebecca a pleasant sense of victory. Marcel asked Lesh if they could please stop now so that he could drink "a lot of sparkling water," and then asked Lesh if he remembered to bring him a "nice piece of dark chocolate."

Rebecca wasn't intimidated by Marcel. This was a new experience for her. She had paid a lot of money for it and she wanted to know. What better way then to ask? She felt entitled to ask whatever questions came into her head even if they were strange ones, like what an elephant thinks about being born. She only wished her students would ask more questions and even ask silly questions if they felt like it.

At their sundown tea that evening, after having witnessed the actual birth of an actual elephant in the actual wild and feeling a bit shocked that these things still happen outside of sanitized hospitals or carefully scrubbed zoos, Rebecca asked Lesh for permission to walk a few hundred yards away from the rover, to stand by an Umbrella Thorn tree that was nearby. He gave her permission and she walked over with her gin and tonic, stood under it and stared at the sun which was quickly dropping to the horizon of distant trees.

There was a large piece of dried elephant dung on the ground which looked like a small soccer ball. She knocked at it with her sneaker, then put her foot on top of it and pushed down. It came apart easily, like shredded wheat cereal, and looked, then, like a mat of dried grass. You'd have hardly thought that it was ever inside an elephant; that it had once been eaten. She turned away from her group and stared at the orange-red sun, which, from this view, hovered a few inches above the tree line on the horizon.

This would have been the place where she would have taken the plastic bag from her back pack and sprinkled her father's remains around the base of this tree, or mix with the elephant dung. The last fragments of her father would have disappeared here. And maybe she would have raised her glass then, and toasted the man who she once called Father — so formal they were. Father. Daughter. She would have walked back and forth across the cremains and helped them find their way into the earth, and the others back by the rover would have seen nothing but the silhouette of a woman strolling casually beneath a tree.

But she didn't have the urn or the bag of ashes, and she didn't want to raise her drink to him. That so-called dream of hers was something fake; something for others. It was just a story she invented. She did feel incredibly unhappy at the time of his death, but it wasn't because he had died. It was because she hated him.

He was a horrible man and she hadn't loved him. She hadn't loved anyone until Julian and it wasn't "hag" love, either, like stupid Bruce The Low had said. Why did that 'hag' word bother her so much? Was Bruce trying to say their relationship wasn't important? Obviously it wasn't sexual love or married love but... well it's some sort of love, she thought. It deserved some respect. All love deserves respect.

She cleared her head of thoughts and looked back at her group — Marcel was ignoring his family, reaching down to the portable tea service set up alongside the back wheel of the Land Rover, to grab another cookie or dark chocolate, or to add more sugar to his tea. She had a sudden change of heart about him. His children, Rebecca decided, were two of the most beautiful and charming children in the world. They stood side by side, holding their cups, staring at her like two little child Gods. Osiris and Isis, Rebecca thought. They smiled and waved at her again and she waved vigorously in return. They made her feel better.

One of the other Americans was walking in her direction. He apparently thought she was waving at him and he waved back, just as broadly, as if the two of them knew each other well and were horsing around. She suddenly remembered with relief that his name was Richard and he approached her with a little chuckle.

"Wasn't that amazing?" he said, "Lesh told me we were extremely lucky to see something like that,"

"I'd say we were," she answered. "If it's all I see on this trip I'll be more than satisfied. But I hope to see more."

"It's so pretty here," he said, turning to stare at the sun, as if it looked different from this place under the tree. "I'm sorry but I forgot your name."

"It's Rebecca. Rebecca Over. Miss."

He grinned, and probably suppressed a laugh, "Mine's Richard Harding. Mister."

She smiled. She didn't feel the need to explain her "Miss," so she didn't. "Is this your first trip to Africa, Richard?" she asked.

"No. I've been here lots of times. Probably ten. But I've never seen an elephant give birth. That was awesome."

She nodded. "I've never seen an elephant give birth either," she said, "and this is my first trip. This is actually my first drive."

"You're incredibly lucky," he said.

She thought for a moment, then said, weakly, "Yes."

She stared back at the sun and Richard stared with her. For a moment, she felt perfectly acute and sharp, as if she was a steel pointer held by an old teacher, who pushed his pointer deeper into the scene, trying to stress a point that no one was getting. *There. There. There.* Pointing at it. *There. There it is students. People all over the world stare at the setting sun. And the moon when it's full. They see it and say, Look at the moon. Regardez la lune. Mira la luna. It's so amazing. And look there's Venus. Let us marvel. That's what she'd say instead of "Let Us Pray."*

She pointed at the evening star and said to Richard, "There's Venus."

"Really?" he asked.

"I've always wished I could have a sunset class with my students so I could show them how to spot Venus or some of the constellations. The sky really doesn't get much attention in school. Clouds do. Atmosphere. But stars are a little neglected I think. But probably if I took my class out on a clear night and said, 'that's the constellation Leo,' they'd run home and tell their parents I was teaching them Satanism."

Richard looked up and seemed incurious about what she had just said. "Interesting," he finally said. "What grade do you teach Rebecca?"

"Seventh."

"Oh boy, that must be a handful. I didn't like seventh grade."

"Oh yes. Yes it is. One of the worst years, I think, but luckily I have a good command of my students. They respect me. I listen to them as often as I can. I think that's why they like me. It's the launching year – launched into the trauma of being a teen. I think it isn't until the boys start maturing that all the problems start. Girls have that short bit of heavenly time when they've matured and they're bigger than the boys. But when the boys catch up, well that's when they all become so cruel to each other, I think. I don't know. I'm mostly earth science. I'm not Piaget."

"That's really interesting." He said this, she thought, like a perfect Midwesterner — not really hearing or meaning what he said.

"The students usually laugh when I tell them that people once thought the earth was flat and rested on the back of a giant turtle, so what I say to them is, 'But would it look different?' And then some of them stop smiling and crease their brows. That's when I can see I'm getting through and making them think. Or contemplate. Maybe that's the better word."

"It must be a really hard job teaching kids."

"It is, if you want them to try. Some of my fellow teachers simply want them to memorize. And some of them want them to learn things that aren't true at all."

"Would you like to sit with us at dinner tonight?" Richard asked.

"Yes. Thank you," she said, feeling flattered.

"It's just that the guy from Belgium is... you know... I have a feeling he wants to talk with me... and I'd rather not talk with him."

She turned and looked back at their group, just as quickly deflated by Richard's need to explain his invite. Marcel was climbing up to the back seat of the vehicle, having a great deal of trouble of pulling himself up to his seat. His wife was standing at the back of the vehicle chatting to Richard's two friends. The two children were still looking in her direction — probably at the place where the sun had just set.

Richard continued, "He asked me what I did and I told him I'm a writer and he immediately asked, 'Are you Dan Brown?' So I said no, I didn't write *The Da Vinci Code*, I'm just a writer for a small Midwestern newspaper, and he cut me off and started telling me how to write a best seller. It turns out that in order to write a bestseller you must 'take zome fictional characteurs and put zem on a mystery zearch.'" Rebecca started to laugh at Richard's impression and because, of course, it was the same story as *The DaVinci Code*.

"'And thees zearch should be a matter of life and death, and it should include zome great artverk by people like.... ummm ummm....,' and then I said to him, 'Leonardo Da Vinci maybe?' and he said, 'No no no, don't be silly. Rembrandt, I think. I have always suspected hidden messages in his work,' and then I said, 'Or we could use De Kooning and call the it *The De Kooning Code*,' and then he frowned at me and popped another piece of chocolate in his mouth and walked away."

"He probably thought you were making fun of his name," Rebecca said,"that's the DeKoning Family. He probably thought you were saying it should be called *The DeKoning Code*."

"Oops," Richard said sheepishly.

They finished their gin and tonics. She suspected they could easily become friends, but she wasn't attracted to him in a physical way, the way she had been attracted to Trevor Wardman until his racism came to the surface.

They walked back to the Land Rover, where silly, plump, Marcel DeKoning sat in the last and highest row, waiting to get going again, like an impatient child strapped into a roller coaster. Rebecca had a sudden desire to shoot him and watch him fall off the back of the truck. She had this odd sense that his wife would turn and look, shrug, and return to her conversation with Richard's friends; that his children would laugh as if it was a cartoon. But that thought passed quickly. She watched, instead, as Marcel raised his camera and focused its enormous lens on Richard and her as they walked toward the rover. She watched that the little chocolate scarfing tyrant steal their picture, but smiled to herself because she suspected his efforts were wasted; for the sun had already set behind them, and it was too dark for pictures.

Chapter 8

At dinner that night, the table was buzzing, and as people do, all those around the table were talking about what had happened that day and the extraordinary sight they had been privileged to witness. Rebecca sat next to Richard and across from his two friends, whose names she was still trying to recall. She had made up an acronym with their initials when they met that morning, MER, but that memory trick didn't take.

The Belgians sat in the middle of the table and at the far end of the table sat Lesh and Felix, both of whom listened with professional passive interest to Marcel's description of the event — a description which seemed to be centered more on Marcel's method than on the event itself.

Richard's friend — Evan, that was it, and Mike — had the same somewhat congenial midwestern appearance as Richard. The three of them, Rebecca decided, were heterosexuals, and all three, she thought, were probably a little lonely and a bit passive when it came to women. But they were interesting enough to take safaris in Africa and, she had learned, trips to see Maachu Pichu and the Polar Bears in Churchill. They were "Eco" tourists.

She enjoyed talking with them over dinner and after recounting of the story of the elephant birth, the conversation gradually turned to other things. It was Evan who asked, "Do you enjoy teaching, Rebecca?"

"Sometimes. Sometimes it's very hard. They've told me not to mention evolution anymore. I don't know what I'm going to do about that, although it was never a big part of the curriculum anyway."

"What do mean?" Richard asked.

"Evolution?" she answered, not sure if Richard wanted to know more about the situation or if he didn't know what evolution was. "My principal has asked — ordered me, actually — not to mention it anymore."

"Are you kidding?" Evan asked.

"I wish I was," she said, "But they've put it into my curriculum — whatever it's called — this Intelligent Design thing. Actually, I'm misstating it. They put nothing into the curriculum, they just took something out."

Felix, at the end of the table, was now listening to Rebecca instead of Marcel, and he piped up and asked, "How so?"

"At the beginning of the semester the principal of my school asked me to schedule an appointment to see him. So naturally I thought it was about a letter I had written to the school board, criticizing them for a contest that had 100 first place winners. But it wasn't. It was to tell me that he didn't want me to mention evolution so as not to offend the —," she used air quotes to emphasize, "religious beliefs of some of the students."

"This is still going on?" Felix asked.

"Yes."

"What was your answer?"

"My answer? It wasn't a debate. He said I would lose my job and I can't afford that."

"So do you think you'll comply?" Richard asked.

"I'm not sure. The curriculum is always changing but it's almost always because of a new discovery or development. This is more like an "undiscovery." I'm not sure what to do. I won't teach Intelligent Design if they put it in. That would be like teaching that there's no God and I can't do that. And I'll tell them that too. If it ever comes to that. You can't make me teach that there's no God."

"But what is this intelligent design anyway?" Elizabeth DeKoning asked. When Rebecca looked at Elizabeth, she noticed that Marcel seemed to be annoyed that Felix was also listening to their conversation.

"The way I understand it, they want to teach that the universe was created by an unspecified intelligence. They say there are things in the universe and life that can only be explained by an intelligent cause, rather than something random. But they don't say that this designer is God, so I don't know who or what it's meant to be. Or where that leaves God. Or they're just lying which is probably closer to the truth."

Felix said, "God's assistant maybe?"

Rebecca shrugged. "I tried to make this point to my principal but his mind is closed. And when someone's mind is closed, it's almost impossible to wrench it open. Like for example, my very best friend in the world is a homosexual and he teaches the fifth grade. But because it's a small town and pretty conservative, he has to keep things quiet or he could easily lose his job if some parent found out and complained. He's got no job protection. But just because people can't see it doesn't mean it's not there. It's there and it has always been there. There have always been homosexuals and they have always had a lot of random sex and a lot of them like to teach too."

Marcel interrupted, "This is not an appropriate conversation to have in front of children."

"Oh I'm sorry Marcel," Rebecca said, "I didn't know they spoke English."

"They don't," his wife Elizabeth said.

"But they understand," he insisted.

"Well I guess what I'm saying — trying to say — is that people do things without knowing why they do them." She stared at her plate of food and seemed to get lost in a thought. But it wasn't a thought that she was having, it was just an image of her father in front of a bowl of soup she had just placed in front of him. The image took her by surprise and she momentarily forgot that she was in Africa.

Marcel took advantage of the pause and said to Felix, "As I was saying..." while Rebecca got rid of the image almost as quickly as it had come and rejoined the table conversation with Richard and his friends for the rest of the meal. She didn't like talking about her principal's plans to change the curriculum because it was upsetting, and she tried to stay quiet for the rest of the dinner.

After eating they settled around a fire pit and swapped stories. Felix had a number of amusing ones to tell about some previous guests, and while he boasted about having easily convinced an entire group of American tourists that there was annual "tree migration" that took place every August, Rebecca stared up at the stars, looked for the Southern Cross and tried to ignore the not very subtle anti-Americanisms. *Please don't offer opinions about the president*, she thought. But just then they heard from somewhere off in the dark, a deep, throaty, "Wooouuuhhh.... wuhh wuhh wuhh wuhh wuhh."

"Listen," Felix said, and they heard it again.

"Wooooouuuhhh.... wuhh wuhh wuhh wuhh wuhh."

"That's the male lion announcing his territory."

It was a magical sound, she thought, one of the "earthiest" sounds she had ever heard, and she breathed deeply. They all listened for more but they heard nothing further and because they all had to get up so early they soon said goodnight and went to their rooms.

Under her duvet, in another extremely comfortable bed, she listened to the nighttime sounds. There were surprisingly few. She could hear Marcel speaking to his wife in their 'tent'. She could hear the clinking of dishes. They must be washing in the kitchen. But there was almost nothing else she could hear until, once again, but much farther away — the lion's "Wooouuuhhh.... wuhh wuhh wuhh wuhh wuhh." She knew from Felix that he was warning other males to get out of his territory, but before she fell asleep, she wondered if it wasn't also to tell his potential meals that he had arrived.

"I am coming to eat you," she said before settling to sleep.

Chapter 9

The next day she said goodbye to Richard, Evan and Mike after breakfast and after getting Richard's address and promising to stay in touch. As this was not the high season, Felix said, there were no new guests coming in, so it was just Rebecca and the DeKonings for the morning drive.

The drive was nothing dramatic like the drive yesterday, but they did, this time, get close to the larger animals; a huge herd of Cape Buffalo; some giraffe; and a pride of lions lying on the ground out in the open. The lions, possibly sisters Lesh said, did absolutely nothing. One of them yawned. But in spite of their lack of activity Rebecca found them fascinating.

Afterwards, back at the camp, Rebecca realized that she was actually starting to relax. She was starting to feel a little bit like those lionesses. She hadn't known that she possessed a certain guardedness — only noticing on the Cessna when she started to cry, and again as the time passed so unhurried on that second day. The hours between lunch and tea. It was impossibly quiet then, as she sat in the lounge with no walls and stared out at a grassy plain that was in front of the camp. It was perfect for reading, but she didn't feel like doing even that small thing. Once, she saw a small herd of impala walk by, nibbling at the ground as they moved forward and they were so quiet you wouldn't have known they were there. There were light blonde young ones with them who ate and moved just as quietly. And then they had passed from her sight. Occasionally, she would see some movement in the grass — or

she'd hear an indistinct human voice from somewhere distant
— usually a woman. Her powerful olfactory sense picked up
the scent of wild sage which grew everywhere, a perfume she
found quite pleasant and made her think of food. She sighed
deeply and realized from the satisfaction behind her sigh that
she was letting go of it — of that defensive posture. Its
abatement — it's dissipation — made itself known to her. It
was like a tense muscle and she wondered as she stared at the
green of grass of the plain, how long she had been that way.
How long and why had she felt the need to guard herself?

There were many possibilities, she thought, many reasons.
Most involving her father. But she decided not to think about
any of her past troubles, but closed her eyes and relished the
peace and quiet, and the agreeable smell of sage that floated all
about her like soothing natural aromatherapy.

She felt that either not much time had passed or that a lot
of time had passed quickly, by the time Marcel DeKoning and
his family entered the lounge. She didn't want to open her eyes
just then and kept them closed while she listened to the family
get tea and drinks from the bar and seat themselves in the
chairs near hers. When she was resigned to socializing, she
opened them and was slightly startled that Marcel was staring
directly at her from the opposite couch.

"Are we disturbing you?" he asked.

"Not at all. I was just enjoying the smell of the air."

"Whatever are you talking about? I smell nothing."

"I have a very keen nose."

Marcel turned to look at his wife and asked, "Ce *qui est ce mot 'keen'?*"

"Sharp," she answered in English.

He turned back to Rebecca and asked, "You have a sharp nose?"

Rebecca laughed inwardly. She didn't hate Marcel. He was ridiculous clown and nothing more. She decided to change the subject. "Are you enjoying the afternoon Marcel?" she asked.

"Yes of course I am," Marcel said, "Please tell me your forename again, I have forgotten it."

"It's Rebecca."

"And what is your family name?"

"Over."

"Over?"

"Yes."

"But how have you come by that name? That is not a proper surname. Listen to me. There are four types of surnames: colors, characteristics, professions or places. Have you studied your background and your pedigree?"

He was also, apparently like her Aunt Vicky, a surname snob. Although she knew perfectly well the origin of her surname and the fact that surnames were derived from five sources (Marcel forgot 'son of'), she decided to lie, in order to displease him.

"No I haven't," Rebecca said, "My father was very circumspect about his background."

"Why? Was he a criminal?"

"No," she laughed, "he worked at the local bank. He was a loan manager."

"It is well known that Americans are the most incurious people of the Third World. Would you like some tea Rebecca?"

"Oh... well yes thank you."

Marcel stood, poured her some tea, carried it over to her sat down again and resumed his insults and flippant observations. But he didn't act as though he meant to be insulting. He was a strange mix.

His wife left the lounge to get the Newman's bird book she had forgotten, and while she was away, Marcel spoke to his children in French even though she knew, from *his* surname, that he was Flemish and could probably just as easily speak Dutch. It was stupid for him to do so because Rebecca spoke French, but she thought probably because she was American and he had a bias about the 'stupid American' he didn't worry that she might know he was changing all her answers for his children.

He told them, for example, that she was a secretary instead of a schoolteacher; and when he asked her what subject she taught, he turned to his children and instead of saying something like, "sciences de la Terre," he said she worked in the "village hospital." Village? Why he did this was beyond her ability to guess, and so before it started to annoy her, she decided to end his interview by asking him what camp was next on their itinerary.

"Mombo," he said.

"Well what a coincidence, so is mine."

*

The following morning, Rebecca and the DeKonings were packed into another Cessna 210 with another cheerful and winsome pilot named Drew. She was beginning to think that bush pilots were the happiest people in the world. They waved goodbye to Felix ("Goodbye Lucky, Mr. Adjective," Rebecca silently said to herself as she waved from the co-pilot's seat) while he watched from the Land Rover, along with four new guests that had just arrived on the same plane. It was the rule that the staff had to stay and make sure the planes departed successfully. They sometimes didn't, Lucky had said.

Chapter 10

Mombo

At the dirt airstrip of their second camp, they were met by one of the assistant managers, a young South African white man in his twenties who introduced himself as Neil, and a Botswanan assistant named Bunte, which they pronounced like "pull me."

They packed their bags into the vehicle and, because Mombo camp was so long, almost a kilometer from one end to the other, Neil dropped the DeKonings and Bunte off at one end, while he drove Rebecca to the other end where her 'tent' was.

The accommodations at this camp made Duba look like a dump. Her room had an indoor and an outdoor shower, a dining table, a long outdoor deck for gazing at the huge green plain in front of her room, a writing table, a private outdoor lounge, an overstuffed bed and ceiling fans. Neil explained as he showed her the room that the camp which was once at a different location on Chief's island, was now entirely built on stilts, so that the buffalo and other animals, when they came through the camp, would walk under the camp rather than through it, as they used to do.

After Neil left, telling her there was about an hour before the afternoon drive, she stepped out onto her deck to stare at her private view. There was a herd of small blond deer-like animals grazing as they slowly walked along the far edge of the field. Some had small curly antlers but others had none at all. Maybe those were the babies. She didn't know what they were called and they didn't notice her as she watched. She clapped her hands once and the entire herd looked up in her direction. After a moment staring, they resumed grazing and she went inside to hang up her clothes.

It took her fifteen minutes to walk the very long length of the elevated boardwalk to get to the lounge. When she arrived, she was surprised at the number of guests — perhaps twenty — most of whom were clustered in little groups. After pouring herself a coffee, Rebecca looked at the clusters of guests and for the first time on this trip, felt awkwardly single. This feeling was actually what had frightened her the most about taking this trip. It was bound to happen.

She scanned the room for the DeKonings, who now felt like her traveling companions — old friends, despite Marcel's personality. She saw no sign of them. A darkly tanned and muscular woman with frizzy blond hair came into the lounge and started rounding up people and sending them off to their vehicles.

"Right," she said, "the Farley family, you're with Aloysius, you know your way, and the Smith family you're with Aloysius also. Aloysius! Aloysius! Raise your hand please so the Smiths know who you are. There he is. Thank you Aloysius!" She directed other people to their guides and then turned to a small clutch of people standing near Rebecca. She said, "Now Beatrice, Alex and Carl I hope you don't mind but you'll be driving with Neil today."

"Why?" the woman named Beatrice asked with an obvious air of defiance.

"Unfortunately Beatrice it's the only way I can fit everyone in with their family or friends you see. I'm so sorry."

Beatrice appeared as an obviously difficult person who had just been "handled." She had short black and gray hair that was held off her face with a colorful headband. Her face was full and rosy and she had a beautiful middle aged woman's figure — one of those people who didn't worry about a few extra pounds. Or so she thought. This was all conjecture. The only thing Beatrice did when the woman in charge apologized for changing their driver was make a kind of sneer and then turned to whisper something in the ear of the man next to her. As they and their driver Neil left for their vehicle, the woman who was assigning cars and guides turned to Rebecca and asked, "Are you Rebecca?"

"Yes,"

"Good. I'm Polly. Assistant manager. I'm so sorry I'm rushed like this. You'll be going about with Quickly today along with John and Sarah and the DeKonings. Are they here?"

"Not yet."

"Oh crumbs," Polly said, "I don't normally do this — if you miss the drive, you miss it, you're responsible for yourselves — but I'll make an exception and run back and see if they're on their way. Be right back. Just a sec. Quickly please wait for me. Thanks there's a chap."

Polly ran from the lounge down the wooden walkway to find the DeKonings. Rebecca again wondered about this favorable treatment they seemed to be getting — why Polly was willing to make an exception for them.

There were just four left in the lounge — Rebecca and the couple Polly had called John and Sarah, and their short Botswanan guide Quickly who was writing on something at the bar. John had a round, darkly tanned face, short tight black hair and it appeared he had forgotten to shave that morning. He was heavy with muscles, but not, it would appear, from lifting weights or some other exercise — rather he looked like someone who lifted heavy boxes for a living or pushed things around. He had the thick hands of a laborer and he was appealing and pleasant to look at.

So was his wife. Sarah was an attractive athletic woman who, like Polly, was also very tan. Her hair was brown, tied back, just like Rebecca's, but not as long. She had thin eyebrows, thin lips and a narrow nose — a somewhat masculine facial structure, Rebecca thought.

"Hello," Rebecca said, "I'm Rebecca Over."

"John Potgieter, and my wife Sarah."

"Pleasure," Sarah said.

"So you're American?" John asked.

"Guilty as charged," she answered.

"And how are you enjoying our fair continent so far?"

"It's been wonderful."

Sarah interrupted, "Can we sit while we wait John?"

They took chairs opposite Rebecca."Actually, I'm glad they switched them out," John said.

"Who?" Rebecca asked.

"Your compatriots. That fellow and his married friends from California. Bloody annoying people, if you don't mind my saying so. I complained about them; said I would not be riding with them in the car. That's why they were changed out. I wasn't sure if they were going to."

"They weren't that annoying..." Sarah said somewhat apologetically, smiling at Rebecca, but Rebecca could sense that Sarah was not exactly in strong disagreement with John's judgment.

"What was annoying about them?"

"That spoiled woman mostly. My bottom hurts," John began, mocking Beatrice, "Do you have a pillow for my bottom Quickly?"

Sarah, at John's side, began to smile. "John," she said, gently rebuking him.

"Christ, you come all the way from California to the heart of bush and all you can worry about is your big fat bum? And did you see her with the sanitizer?" he asked his wife, who nodded patiently. "Constantly rubbing that shit all over her hands? Americans are so full of superstitions it's coming out their ears." He looked back at Rebecca and realized. "Sorry," he said.

To get off the subject of Americans Rebecca asked, "Are you both from South Africa?"

"I'm from Cape Town," Sarah said.

"Zimbabwe originally," John said, "'til that fucking bastard took our land and gave it to his cabinet ministers."

"Are you talking about Mugabe?" Rebecca asked.

"It's best not to bring up the subject," Sarah answered before John was able to answer. John's facial expression indicated that he agreed – that he didn't want to get started about Mugabe. He was intense, Rebecca felt, and very masculine. She wondered what he looked like without clothes and the thought made her grin. John noticed Rebecca's smile and grinned back at her which she thought was sort of funny given the thought that was behind it. What if he could read her mind?

Just then the DeKonings were brought into the room by Polly and introduced to John and Sarah. Their guide Quickly took them to their vehicle. Rebecca sat in the lower row, next to John. Sarah was on his other side. Marcel was, as usual, in the upper row — but alone because his wife and children took the middle row. While they bounced slowly along on the extremely dusty drive, doing the long slow search to find an animal to look at, stopping once to watch a small family of wart hogs, and again to watch some giraffe loping along, Rebecca began to feel very lonely.

This drive was turning out to be slower and longer than the others had been. Maybe it was just that she had gotten used to the scenery so it wasn't as new. But they weren't spotting anything — not even any birds.

They had been driving for nearly half an hour. The sun beating down was hot, and she leaned forward and spoke to their guide as he drove. "Quickly," she asked, "Do you think it's too hot for the animals to be out?" "Ahhhhh," he said, and then added, "mmmmm." He turned and smiled at her. She repeated her question but all Quickly said was, "Mmmmm."

She leaned back in her seat, no wiser, and John, sitting next to her, said, "I reckon it is too hot. Another fifteen minutes they'll start to come out. Same as yesterday, except yesterday we had a bird named Beatrice with us who did nothing but complain about the heat and her arse." Rebecca smiled weakly, already a little tired of hearing complaints about this person she had never met, and continued to stare at the land as they drove through it.

The guidebook she had consulted said that this delta was really a desert, part of the vast Kalahari, which was so barren and flat it was said you could stand at night, alone, and see in all four directions nothing but stars from horizon to horizon — a place where you could count exactly three things: the stars, the earth and yourself — or four if the moon was out. But here, where the Okavango River flowed so slowly that the water took months to travel only a few hundred miles, the land was transformed into something lush. Rain only came for two months of the year — usually about October to December — but by January the water that rained in Angola had come down to Botswana's Inland Delta, arriving in an event everyone called "The Flood."

She noticed that everyone: the guides, the managers, the residents of Maun and know-it-all tourists like Marcel had talked about "The Flood" this year or "The Flood" next year or last. Listening to the people talk about "The Flood" Rebecca began to get a sense of how it might have been that primitive societies were able to create gods out of the land around them because with all the talk about "The Flood" they could just as easily have been using a proper name to describe the same thing. "When Flood comes He will turn the land green." That saying would turn into "When Florn comes," and then it would be Fjorn... and then suddenly a River God is born. There was something mystical and ancient about listening to these people talk about the yearly flood. They were creating a God.

She began, unexpectedly, to tear up, and she turned her head to wipe her eyes. She wished she could have seen this when she was younger, in her twenties. But she sometimes felt she had been robbed of her youth, robbed of it by her father, and at certain unusual times, like right now, this feeling of having been robbed asserted itself and overcame her.

She took a breath to clear away her feelings. A crackling came over the vehicle's intercom which Quickly answered. He exchanged a few words which Rebecca could not understand, and then suddenly stepped on the gas and sped off at a much faster pace. Their accents had been difficult to interpret, so John asked, "What did he say?"

Quickly shouted while pointing in a vague way, "The hyenas are just over there. They are going to kill."

They were racing along a dirt road next to a small grove of trees and all the passengers held on as best they could. It was very bumpy and Rebecca turned to look back at the storm of dust they were leaving in their wake. As she had her head turned, John looked at her and grinned.

"Everyone wants to see a kill," he shouted, "that's why most of them come." After a moment, he reconsidered, and shouted, "... and to see the birds." Rebecca smiled, but as they continued racing along the dirt path to whatever place Quickly had in mind, she thought that it certainly wasn't the reason she came all this way. In fact she hadn't even thought about "a kill" and wasn't sure she wanted to see one. But she swallowed her anxiety and held on as Quickly drove the Land Rover in a way that suited his name.

They rounded the far edge of a clutch of trees, and slowed the vehicle a bit. A few hundred yards away, one of the other safari vehicles was parked and, from what Rebecca could see, the other guests at the camp all had their eyes and cameras trained on something that was between the two vehicles. "Is it already over?" Sarah asked. "No," Quickly said. Quickly took the vehicle much closer, about fifty yards from the other vehicle, then slowed and stopped. He shut off the engines, turned to his passengers and spoke in a whisper. "There," he said, pointing to a small harem of impala that were walking slowly in front of a clump of bushes. About twenty in number, they were smaller than deer, and all of them were female except for the single male to whom this harem belonged. With most of the impala were light colored babies, about three quarters the size of their mothers.

Rebecca turned around to look at Anton and Griet to see how they were doing. They appeared curious but otherwise not too anxious. They strained their necks to get a look. Behind them their father had his camera equipment ready and he had already fired off a few twicks.

She looked back at Quickly and was about to lean forward to ask a question about the babies, but just before she could, the hyenas came bursting out of the bushes, making a horrible screeching sound. She jumped back as the entire herd of impala instantly fled through the large gap between the two vehicles. Their hooves thumped against the ground like muted drums and she could feel the stampede in her entire body. The hyenas caught one of the baby impala that had been closest to where they had come running out, and they were on it in an instant.

Closer to the other vehicle than their own, the baby struggled to get away and tried to keep its head up as it was brought down by the cackle. It looked uncertain as to what was happening as it was slaughtered. Even before it was dead, one of the hyenas tore off its hind limb, and ran away carrying the leg in its mouth like a prize. Amid screams and shrieks and the strange hyena laugh, the other four animals tore the baby apart as if it was made of paper and sticks, turning it to shredded meat and blood in an instant. The entire kill took no more than a minute, and the hyenas settled in to eating hurriedly, squabbling hideously, and attempting to steal each other's spoils like greedy thieves. One of them was already eating the bones, crushing them like hard candy, while another was carrying the baby's head in its mouth to a more distant area. The neck was shredded and dripping blood; the large eyes in the head were black and unreflective. A vulture landed nearby but it didn't look like it was going to be able to steal anything, and it didn't try.

It was the twik twik twik of Marcel's rapid fire camera that brought Rebecca back from wherever she had gone while the kill took place. While it happened, she felt all the blood drain from her face and couldn't move. Everything in her wanted to scream, but an equally strong part of her was immobilized, just as she would be in a nightmare. Now that it was over, she was beginning to feel her face again, the circulation of her blood, and her breath. She hadn't taken a single picture.

She turned around to look at the children. They seemed far less upset than she expected. They turned in tandem and looked at Rebecca, but didn't smile as they usually did, and then looked back at the grim feast. Their eyes were moist, and then Griet, who was sitting between her brother and mother, reached for her mother's arms and started to cry into them. Elizabeth stroked her back.

Rebecca heard a loud sob coming from the other vehicle. She looked over and saw that the California woman — Beatrice — who had so annoyed her fellow passenger was sobbing onto the chest of one of the men with her arm covering the exposed side of her head. The other member of their party — a short oddly tanned man with glasses — was standing in the higher row behind them, and seemed to be pointedly ignoring them as he continued to take pictures of the kill. The guide, the same Neil who had picked her up at the airstrip, kept turning around to look at Beatrice with a scowl, as if she would see his disapproval and quiet herself. The rest of the passengers didn't seem as agitated about Beatrice as he did, and like the people in her own vehicle, they stared at the hyenas and the remnants of what had been a baby impala, and photographed the dining animals.

Rebecca looked to her right, over at the herd. They had moved off, but not very far — not as far as one would think they should. But apparently they knew or understood that the danger was over. There wouldn't be another attack for awhile. What she took to be the mother of the baby stepped back and forth at the front edge of the herd, looking back at the hyenas, as if still hoping there was a chance for her child to make it to safety. But safety, in this case, was the sacrifice made by her own child: a child to satisfy the hunger of the starving hyenas. Another thought crossed Rebecca's mind about the horrible practice of human sacrifice and the need for Gods to be satiated, but she lost it when John spoke up.

"It was fucking murder," he said, "that's all it was."

Rebecca was surprised to see that he was so visibly upset. His lip was trembling and she thought that if he wasn't a man and trying to hold it in, he might be as distraught at Beatrice over in the other vehicle. Sarah took his hand and squeezed it. "It's alright John," she said. He wiped his eyes and kissed his wife and with that and a deep breath seemed to clear his feelings. He put his arm around her shoulder and looked at Rebecca and smiled.

"Murder I tell you," he said.

In the other vehicle Beatrice started screaming at Neil who put his two hands in the air as if in surrender and turned to face forward and away from her. She had her finger pointed at the back of his head, as if she was scolding him. Her husband maintained his contact with his hand on her shoulder, but he didn't try to stop her. She was leaning forward, aggressively.

"Do you hear me Neil?" she yelled. "Don't you ever fucking say that to me!" Her husband gently pulled her back then and she curled up against his chest and continued to cry for the impala baby.

"I wonder what that's all about?" John said to no one in particular.

Quickly turned and explained to his group a bit about the hyenas.

"They don't like to hunt," he said, "but they do sometimes. They eat, usually... emmmm.... caddeun? Caddeun?"

John said, "Carrion?"

"Yes," Quickly said, "They eat, usually, caddeun. They eat anything. Anything at all. Even if it's r-r-rotting they will eat it. Sometimes, after a death, they will dig up a body and eat it. Even something that is three days dead, and buried in the ground; they will dig him up and eat him."

"You're joking!" John said.

"No R'ra, I am not," Quickly said. "And those ones, they are the females? Yes? And she and her sisters, they are at the center of the pack. Yes? They are the leaders? And she is the only one who will mates. All the other ones are aunties. Yes, and the males, they are always on the edge or by themselves because the females, they don't like the males. They hate the males. So the males are sometimes, all alone. Some of them they never get to mates for the whole life. And they used to think that the hyenas could change the sex? See? Because the female has a the same... genital... as the male."

"Seriously?" Sarah asked with a smile.

"Yes they do not know why, but the female will grow the false teste, and she look just like a man from the outside." He pointed to the dominant female, "If she walk around there, that one — if she walk around you can see the two blue uhhh — r-r-r-round. Those is the false teste."

"But she's still a female?" Elizabeth asked.

"Yes M'ma. But she look like a male."

Rebecca had a question. "Quickly, are the hyenas related to wolves?"

"No M'ma," Quickly said, "They are like the cats. But they are their own... ummm... specie. So they are different from the other animals. They are alone. They are very very ugly. Very ugly. But they eat anything, even the bones, even the copse in the ground. So they are not the endangered specie like the cheetah or the wild dogs. They will eat... anything. They will do anything. Anything anything anything. Yes that is why." His voice trailed off in an unfinished thought.

"They'll probably still be here to eat all of us when the end comes," John said, but Rebecca couldn't tell if he was joking and he didn't smile.

They were ugly creatures, just as Quickly said. They had coarse hair and strange sloping rears, and their eyes were dull and filmy. Cold eyes. They were machine-like in their eating and they made all sorts of crazy screams and calls, plus the odd laughing sound that they were named for, that made her think of lunatics at some sort of hillside blood festival or something. It was clear that by the time they were done, there would be nothing left of the baby impala except a patch of bloody grass. Not even a bone would be left.

She heard the other Land Rover start its engine and looked up to see that Beatrice had stopped crying and now lay with her head on her husband's shoulder. She watched Neil pick up the radio mouthpiece and call their vehicle. Quickly answered and Neil explained that "one of his pax" wasn't feeling well and suddenly thought she might be coming down with malaria. "I don't know if it's malaria but she's got something wrong with her for sure," he said.

Beatrice must have heard because she sat up and screamed at Neil again, "What the hell is that supposed to mean?" They didn't need the radio to hear her shouting from just thirty yards away. Neil didn't move a muscle as Beatrice continued to berate him from her row behind and above him. "You have no right. You have no right. I *am* sick. I have malaria or sleeping sickness. Something's wrong with me. You have absolutely no right to judge me, you fucker!"

Neil picked up the radio again, and told Quickly that he was just going to run her and her husband back to camp, so that she could have "an aspirin and a lie down." Neil's tone was still intensely sarcastic, but he used no mocking words that would further upset Beatrice. Quickly promised to radio him if anything else happened.

After they left, Rebecca looked over at the herd of impala which still grazed quietly close to the place where they had stopped running, as if nothing had occurred. The mother was no longer waiting for her baby. She had forgotten about it and had disappeared into the blond blend of the herd. She was forced to, Rebecca supposed, feeling a bit chilled by the thought, because there wasn't anything to say and no way of understanding. All that mother knew, if one was going to try to translate the thoughts of a female impala was, *"Once I had a baby. Then it was gone."*

Chapter 11

At drinks that night, Rebecca noticed that one of Beatrice's companions — the short man — was sitting alone by the fire, staring at it with what she thought was a strangely glum expression. He had sat behind the other two so she suspected he was single. She moseyed over to where he sat and said, "I see you're enjoying the fire."

He looked up, surprised. "Yes, I love fires."

"I'm Rebecca Over."

"Carl Baldwin."

"And what part of the world do you call home?"

"Do you know Russian River?"

"No, but by your accent I'm guessing it's not in Russia."

Carl laughed insincerely and said, "Northern California. It's beautiful. And you?"

"Ohio. Northern Ohio. And it's also beautiful but only in the summer. In the winter it's so dreary it's often very depressing. Very gray. The sky looks like clay all the time. She sat in the chair next to Carl as she continued. "But I've lived there all my life and I've never had the money or the inclination to move to a nicer climate."

"But how can you afford... well... sorry that's none of my business," Carl said.

"How can I afford this trip? I received a small inheritance."

"Oh," he said, but he didn't probe any further, just added, "It's unbelievably expensive."

There was a short awkward pause as they both stared at the fire. It was as if Carl was deciding whether or not to talk about himself. He finally said, "I always wanted to take a safari. This is my life long dream. The one thing I wanted to do before I died. Bucket list kind of thing. I had to save for... five years I think. I love animals. I love animals more than people. But I had to figure out the right people to invite, and you know, Alex and Beatrice — we've been really close friends for such a long time. I mean I could have asked a friend to come, you know, but it just had to be the right people because this is my dream. You know? I don't want it ruined. And they're even more into nature than I am. They've completely eliminated plastic from their lives. They recycle everything. No air conditioning ever. They're trying to have a zero footprint. I couldn't go that far. I need air conditioning."

Rebecca nodded but as he continued to awkwardly tell the story of his friendship with Alex and Beatrice, she noticed there was something in the way Carl looked that wasn't quite right. His hair was cropped at the very closest setting — she'd seen a number of balding men with that close-clipped look and he was very well tanned, but his face was oddly flushed. There was also something about his eyes that looked both sad and angry. And with the way he kept insisting too many times that this was "his trip of a lifetime" and "very special to me" and that he "didn't want it ruined," she suddenly realized that Carl was dying and she suspected drug resistant AIDS.

It made her want to talk with him more and get into an even deeper conversation about their lives, but before she could make a gentle probe into the state of his health, the camp's manager came over and interrupted by introducing himself.

"Are you Rebecca?" he asked. He carried a drink of what looked to be whisky.

"Yes," she said, standing.

"Excuse me please," Carl said, "I've got to get something from my room," and he left.

"We haven't met yet. I'm Scott Wilson, the camp manager here. Why don't you sit at my table for dinner tonight?"

"I'd be happy to," Rebecca said.

"Good," he said pointing at the open air dining room, "My table's the center one and I sit at this end. Sit at the seat to my left," and then he walked over to another group of people.

She sighed, slightly annoyed that she had been interrupted for such a stupid instruction, but she supposed she should consider it an honor. She sat down again and stared at the fire by herself. Carl's health was none of her business of course, but she felt sympathy for him.

For her own business she had kept so close to herself and at the same time, so far away from herself, that no one would ever suspect she even had her own business to tell. And it was, for a reason unknown to her, asserting itself on this trip. She had manipulated that whole awful part of her life into a blind spot that the eye of her mind could not see and did not have to look at. Even with Julian she had never broached the subject, fearing that he shared the opinion of Bruce The Low that women who aborted were not "natural women." But at that moment, just before the interruption, while Carl was talking about how special this experience was for him and how he didn't want Beatrice ruining it, she had great sympathy for Carl. He was dying and didn't want to.

Of course there was nothing unusual in that, if it was even the case, but why were these thoughts about her own past intruding now? When she hadn't thought about the matter in ages? It was as if the subject was coming out from behind a cloud and she needed to find someone to talk to about it. Her first urge to tell someone was Richard at the other camp, and now again with Carl she had wanted to go off together and talk. But Richard wasn't the right person and any further familiarity with Carl had been cut short by Scott Wilson, Big Shot Manager.

She looked over at Scott, who was listening to some other guests and looked professionally interested in whatever they had to say. Scott was strawberry blonde and pale with freckles. He looked like he wasn't meant to be in the sun and he was just a tad overweight. But he carried himself with great authority. He stood like a soldier at ease, with his legs firmly apart and his hands clasped behind his back. He leaned forward to listen carefully. She thought that he was probably quite proud to be the manager of this camp — the best in the delta, Marcel had said.

At the dinner table later, she did as she was instructed and sat to Scott's left. John and Sarah sat opposite her and next to them was Neil. Others at the table were Quickly, the DeKoning Family, and at the far end were Alex, Beatrice and

Carl. Rebecca had a good view of Beatrice and she didn't look well at all. She looked like she wasn't recovering from the emotionally wrenching afternoon.

At all of the camps in the Delta the evening meal was introduced by one of the Botswanan cooks. At Mombo this was a tiny and thin woman named Drops. Scott explained that she was named Drops because she had been dropped on her head right after being born. She had a very high pitched voice, and when she announced the meal, Rebecca closed her eyes and imagined she was listening to a little budgie or a Love Bird. It was almost like that awful character in *Gone With The Wind*, but nicer to listen to — a very sweet sound as opposed to grating.

"Good evening, ladies and gentlemen," Drops chirped.

"Good evening Drops,'" the guests replied in unison. This was another tradition that seemed to be universal among the camps: the guest responses.

"Tonight we have prepared a very special meal for you."

"Oooh," the chorus said.

"First, we have almonds and gr-r-r-een beans."

"Mmmmm."

"Next we have gem squash."

"Mmmmm."

"Then we have r-r-r-oasted new potatoes."

"Mmmmm."

"Next is cauliflower."

"Mmmmm."

"And for the main we have a r-r-r-roasted leg of lamb."

"Mmmmm."

"Thank you. Tonight, we will ask for the ladies first."

"Thank you Drops," Scott said loudly, "Ladies, please help yourselves."

The women all rose and made their way to the serving table where the food was presented. Rebecca found herself in line behind Beatrice, who, she noticed, only took a dollop of each vegetable dish. She took no meat and returned to her seat but did not start eating. When Rebecca returned to the table Scott said loudly for all the women to hear, "Ladies please start, don't wait for the boys." As Rebecca started eating her gem squash, she noticed that Beatrice was not even looking at her food, but sat with her fingers under her chin and stared at a spot to her right, with her eyes unfocused.

When the women were seated and the men rose to get their meals, Scott remained seated and Rebecca asked him, "Aren't you eating?" He said, "After the guests," and then said to the women and one girl at his table,"So I heard you were quite lucky today."

"It wasn't luck," Beatrice snapped loudly before anyone else could answer. She had not turned her head to speak to Scott and continued to stare off at that blank spot to her right. Neil was at the serving table when she said this and Rebecca saw him snap his head around. She watched him as carefully as she watched her more mischievous students while he finished piling his plate with food and returned to the table. As he passed behind Beatrice he subtly sneered at the back of her head, then looked around for a cohort with which he could share the joke, but found none. She recognized what was happening. If this was her classroom one or two of the boys was about to start picking on one of the girls. Neil was sitting three seats away from Beatrice, and Rebecca thought that it was probably a good thing there was a buffer.

Beatrice's angry response stopped any replay of the kill from taking place, but not for very long, because it was, of course, the one thing that everyone wanted to talk about. Witnessing a kill was like the jewel in the crown of a photographic safari and it was undeniable that there was a deep sense of satisfaction in the dining room, at all the tables. She had felt it earlier in the lounge before dinner: an excitement and jubilance that had everyone feeling flushed, or as if they had accomplished something.

Rebecca had sympathy for Beatrice — but it was no greater than her sympathy for those who found the kill exciting. She was somewhere right in the middle between nature at its bloodiest and civilization at its most shrink-wrapped and sanitized. It was probably one of those things that people want to explain, but really can't. To say 'it's just nature' was like saying, 'it's the weather' or 'it's an act of God'. It's out of our hands. It's beyond our understanding. It's happening elsewhere in places I can't see.

But at the same time, Rebecca thought, we do care about the things we see, and we react to them in whatever way we are prone. It's not possible to say, 'well, if I wasn't here I wouldn't have seen it and wouldn't be upset about it now'. What Beatrice saw was the cold blooded killing of a completely defenseless baby animal. The real horror of being alive, Rebecca thought, was that the soft and cool values of intelligence and empathy didn't matter. The only thing that really mattered was the harsh hot fact of hunger and eating and here they all were, sharing the leg of a lamb that someone had killed. They were all eating — everyone except Beatrice, who wasn't even eating her poor innocent vegetables.

Scott asked Marcel if he was able to take any good pictures that day and Marcel perked up at being able to talk about himself again. He was clearly some sort of nature photographer and did this yearly. He began to tell Scott of all the remarkable shots he had taken, describing in casual detail about the baby Impala's head in the mouth of one of the hyenas being carried away and other gruesome aspects of the kill until Beatrice said, almost shouting, "I hope they all go extinct."

Neil leaned forward to look at her to say, quite angrily but not shouting, "Oh come on Beatrice, it's nature. That's just mother nature at work. That's what this is all about. That's why you've come here. It's the natural world. You can't argue with the natural world."

"Yes I can!" she shouted, "they're vicious animals and I hope every single one of them dies. I hope they get some disease or a dog virus."

"They're not part of the dog family," Neil said.

"I don't care. I hope they completely disappear off the face of the planet."

"Well they're not bloody likely to do that, seeing as how they're one of the fiercest and strongest animals on earth."

"Neil," Scott said, interrupting and warning him, but he wasn't dissuaded by his boss.

"They have to eat too," he continued, lecturing Beatrice, "You'd be just as upset to see them all turned to skin and bones and starving to death. Have you ever seen an animal starve Beatrice? It's a hundred times worse than a hunt I can tell you that."

"I'd be thrilled to see those things starve to death!"

Her husband tried to interrupt, "Beatrice, honey, please..."

"I'd give them all poison if I could, or cyanide. That's what I'd do."

"You know, where the hell do you bloody fucking ignorant Americans..."

"Neil!" Scott barked. "Would you please ask Drops to bring out the butter?"

Neil looked at Scott, and then at Rebecca briefly, before looking down at the butter dish that was sitting immediately in front of Scott's plate. Neil's face sank as he watched Scott conspicuously take a large scraping of butter and spread it on a piece of bread. Scott looked at Neil once more as he took a bite and said, "Thanks, mate. She must have left it in the fridge." Neil, reprimanded and looking embarrassed, stood and quietly left the table. He walked to the kitchen area in the back, behind the table of food, without a departing word to anyone. Rebecca looked across at John and Sarah, who both seemed as uncomfortable as she was, although she had the keenest sense that John might have been suppressing a smile.

"It's not a very good explanation," Scott said to Beatrice but for the benefit of all the guests, "but you were hitting a raw nerve. Neil has a great fondness for the hyenas. He's actually writing a book about them."

"What!" Beatrice said, "a book about those horrible animals!?" She stood suddenly, as if standing strengthened her argument. She pointed out "there" in the dark where the hyenas lived, while she yelled at Scott, who was clearly unmoved by her tirade and had decided it was best to let her scream. "That poor innocent baby deer did nothing to deserve what those things did to it. He was just an innocent child, standing next to his mother and the way they ripped him apart like that... just... ripped..." She choked up and started crying as she saw it in her mind once more. She covered her mouth and walked over to the open side of the room behind Scott, stared out at the dark and sobbed.

The guests at all three tables sat in silent embarrassment. Rebecca couldn't eat while this was happening. Beatrice appeared to stop herself, place her hands on her stomach, breathed deeply a few times, then turned and walked back to the table. Tears covered her cheeks. She said to her husband, "Alex, I think I'm just going to go to bed."

Scott jumped to his feet, "I'll be happy to walk you there Beatrice."

"I'm alright, I can walk myself."

"No. No. I'm sorry..." he started to say, but then she interrupted, "God dammit, I said I can walk myself, Scott!"

"I heard you Beatrice, and I'm very sorry, but it's company policy. We walk guests back to their tents when it's dark. Lions can and do come into the camp at night and sometimes they walk along the walkway. Do you have your torch?"

Rebecca had to admit to herself that Scott was good at being in charge. Beatrice made no more arguments and he left holding her by the elbow and guiding their way along the raised walkway with a flashlight, or torch, as he called it. After they were gone, the rest of the guests ate quietly in the dim candlelight. Beatrice had called the animal an innocent child which reminded Rebecca of the protestors at the clinic.

Fortunately, before she could think about all of that, the small talk at all three tables started again, and the romance of eating a fantastic meal outdoors, in the heart of Africa, reasserted itself. Neil returned from the back with a couple bottles of wine for everyone, "his treat" he said, and he seemed completely undisturbed about having been reprimanded and sent to the back like a misbehaving child.

After some time, Scott returned. The drama was all forgotten and everyone remarked on how delicious the lamb and veggies were. Drops appeared later to present two different desserts and several types of cheese, after which some of the guests went to their rooms and the others removed themselves to the fire pit, to sit around the fire with coffee or tea, or to drink beer, and to lose themselves by staring at the flames.

Scott quietly mentioned to those around the fire that Beatrice and her party would be leaving tomorrow morning.

They had already been informed and arrangements were already being made.

"You're throwing them out?" Rebecca asked.

"We can't have guests behaving that way. We'll probably be sued but it's less harm than having everyone else's vacation ruined."

"But it's Carl's lifelong dream." She said this almost as if it were her own dream being ruined. "It was just one outburst."

Scott shrugged, which she thought was cruel. She thought about how Carl's dying wish — his trip of a lifetime was now dashed and about how disappointed he must now feel. Would their friendship survive this? He picked them because of their environmental beliefs, but out here, Beatrice couldn't take it. The cruelty — or the horror. Whatever it was. This is what so many people thought with regard to California "hippies" — that they were soft and spoiled. Not real survivors.

When they heard the first *wuh wuh wuh* of a lion as he began his territorial stakeout, Scott explained that the lion was quite a long way off, possibly even a couple of miles away, but that his voice was so powerful, it could travel the entire distance of his territory. His voice, Scott said, was his way of establishing territory. She had already heard this from Felix at the other camp.

"Does that mean we are in his territory?" Rebecca asked.

"Yes," Scott said, "for now."

And then they were silent.

"Every meal begins with a weapon," John said, "and for animals it's their teeth, isn't it?"

Several people nodded in agreement.

They sat in silence for a bit more, and listened to the lion calling several more times, but always far away. Something occurred to her then; a thought she had at the other camp when she heard the lions off in the distance.

"Scott?"

"Yes."

"How do you know that he's not speaking to us?"

They all turned to look at Rebecca. She could see John and Sarah smiling. Scott was smiling too, but his smile was condescending, as if he was amused.

"Well I guess we just have to assume he doesn't know English," Scott said.

He said this with a subtext that she should stop talking. She didn't like Scott. He was condescending and too proud. The way he boasted about throwing them out. He probably didn't have to, and why did he have to tell anyone? He probably disliked women in general.

But in spite of Scott's attempt to shut her up, Sarah held her head slightly skewed, as if truly curious about what Rebecca had just asked. And John had leaned forward holding his beer with two hands. The smoke that was blowing in his direction didn't seem to bother him.

"Obviously Scott I don't mean that he's speaking English or French. What I mean is that what if his call is a way of telling the living things in his territory that they *belong* to him? Like ownership. What if his need to roar is what a farmer does when he talks to his pigs or clucks at his chickens, all the animals he knows he's going to kill one day? What if that lion's just walking around reassuring everyone that we're all safe tonight and that tonight we're not going to become his food? Tomorrow, maybe, but not tonight. He's our owner."

Scott nodded, as if considering her thought, but she could see he was annoyed at having to listen to it. The looks from the others around the fire were confused, but Sarah said, "What a lovely way of thinking about it," and John added, "I rather like that," and gave her a big smile which made him look warm and kind and very attractive, she couldn't help thinking.

There was more chat, and Scott, somehow relating it to Beatrice, told a story about an American client who refused to believe that an ostrich had a brain, and wondered how someone so ignorant could have the money to take a trip to Africa, or why they would want to.

"But you didn't give her the money back, did you? For being ignorant I mean?" Rebecca asked.

"Oh no," Scott said, "it's the Americans that keep us in business. And the Japanese. And one good thing you can say about the Americans is they are as social as anyone can be. They're always happy to meet new people. In fact it's something they seem to need. The Japs don't socialize with anyone at all. They stick to themselves in small little packs. The Germans are the most trouble. They never listen. Most animal attacks here in Bots happen to Germans because they don't listen. Or they don't care, maybe. I don't know. Either way, you tell them they must not get out of the vehicle unless given permission but that means nothing. They want to get a better picture, they get out of the vehicle, the hippo charges, and then they're cooked. Sauer later Kraut."

"Hippos?" she asked, ignoring his idiotic joke.

"The hippopotamus is the most dangerous animal in Africa. More people are killed by hippos than any other animal. If you go into any of the villages in the Delta or even in Maun after the flood comes you often see the locals shouting at the hippos in the river. They're easily provoked, very suspicious and territorial and you should see how fast they can run. Shoo! They're a member of the horse family you know. I once saw one running in the daytime and I figured that fat thing was clocking at something like forty kilometers an hour. So that's why you don't get out of the vehicle and why we walk you to your rooms. This isn't Disneyland here. It's not safe. People actually die sometimes and then we have to get Sefofane out here to fly their bodies out wrapped in sheets. Not a nice way to end your trip."

Chapter 12

The other guests around the fire soon excused themselves and were walked back to their tents by either Scott or Neil. Soon, only Scott, John, Sarah and Rebecca remained, and Rebecca suspected that Scott didn't want to stay but only stayed because it was his job. He told another story about a Saudi Arabian princess that had booked the entire camp for herself and her staff, then left after an hour because she was bitten by a Tse Tse fly, but Rebecca wasn't paying attention because she involuntarily thought again of the hyenas and the Impala and Beatrice's reaction about the "innocent deer" that they killed which was simply nature and neither innocent or guilty.

An old joke of Mark Twain's suddenly came back to her and she giggled aloud.

"What are you laughing about over there?" John asked, grinning widely at her. Not that she was counting, but John was on his second after-dinner beer and had drunk two before dinner, and a glass or two of wine during it. But he seemed quite lit up; one of those people who are energized by drinking rather than turned dull or angry by it.

"It was just a joke I remembered of Mark Twain's," she said.

"So let's have it then," he said.

"Well I don't remember anything except the punchline," she said, "so I'll have to make it up with apologies to Mark Twain. So let's see. A man who was living in a small town was reading the National Geographic one day about a tribe of cannibals in the middle of South America. He was disgusted when he read that they ate the brains of other human beings. Couldn't sleep. Couldn't rest. It bothered him constantly. Suddenly one day he had a vision from God. God told him that he was supposed to travel to the place where the cannibals lived, and bring them the word of God, because this would stop them from eating human flesh. So the man became a missionary and he traveled all the way to South America and finally found the cannibals that he'd read about and he began to preach to them. He preached the word of God and he preached the love of Jesus Christ and the path to salvation. And the cannibals listened very carefully to everything the missionary had to say. And then they ate him."

The four roared with laughter together, and she felt happy with herself for having given something funny to this couple that she liked, courtesy of Mark Twain. Then John added his own story to the mix, because he collected Bushman stories, he said. Or what he meant, rather, was that he liked to read about the Bushman stories that had been collected a hundred plus years ago, but were now mostly forgotten. The stories were relics of an extinct culture, like fragments of ancient pottery.

"A lot of the stories involve this little Bushman character named Heiseb," John explained, "He's a kind of Everyman in the culture. In the Khoi culture you would go over to your neighbor's to have a smoke and a chat and you would tell stories about Heiseb. And it was okay to make up new stories because the Bushmen believed that stories were brought to them by the wind.

"So did the wind bring you this story John?" Rebecca asked.

"Yes," he said, "absolutely. I don't know how I got into this folklore or mythology or whatever it is, except that the Potgieters have been in Africa since the founding of Cape Town, about twelve or thirteen generations I think — same age as New York City actually — I've always loved Africa. But the Bushmen especially. The people of the Kalahari. This one's about the bee, which is a symbol for knowledge or wisdom in African culture."

So one day, John began, *Heiseb lay down on a bed of soft green grass, and stared up at the night sky which was full of stars. He took his finger and pointed at the sky and started to count them. And hours and hours went by, until he had counted them all. Then after he had counted all the stars he shut his eyes and fell into a deep sleep. The next day no one could wake him. And he slept that way for many years. One group of people began to think that Heiseb was no longer alive. And another group of people said yes, Heiseb is still alive. And a third group of people wished that everyone else would be quiet and stop talking about Heiseb. And then a fourth group of people said the man sleeping in the desert wasn't Heiseb at all.*

And so it came to pass that all these groups began to fight with each other. At first they fought only with words and expressions, but they were unsatisfied and began to fight with their fists and sticks and clubs. Soon after that, they were unhappy with just bruising and maiming, so they began to kill each other. But even with all the killing, Heiseb slept through all of it. Finally all the fighting was done, and there was only one man left. This man looked around, and seeing only the sleeping body of Heiseb on the ground, realized that he was the last murderer. So, seeing no one else to murder, he murdered himself, by hanging himself from a tree. And his body slowly shrank and turned hard and that is why the sausages hang from the Sausage tree. Because for a long time, that was the last man.

And Heiseb never stirred.

While he slept, the grass beneath him began to dry, and it turned brown and died. And then all the trees that surrounded Heiseb dried up and died. Then the termites came and ate all the dead trees. And then the shrubs and bush dried up, and when a fire came through, all the shrubs and bush were turned into black smoke and grey ashes which mixed with the dust and blew away. And then the river stopped flowing and the rain stopped falling. And all the animals had to leave Heiseb's side, because he would not wake.

Finally, there was only Heiseb left alone in the entire world, lying flat on his back in the middle of the desert, with nothing around him at all.

And for many hundreds of seasons this was.

And Heiseb would not wake.

And for many thousands of years this was.

And Heiseb would not wake.

Now one day, after all these thousands of years had passed, and no one anywhere remembered anything about what the world was like before Heiseb went to sleep, a Bee got lost, and he saw, far off in the distance, lying in the hot sun in the middle of the desert, the small naked figure of a dark little man. This was Heiseb. So the Bee flew over to see if this desert sleeper could give him directions. When he arrived at Heiseb, he buzzed all about and inspected him. Heiseb's skin was dark and his hair was black and curly, and he was covered with desert dust from the thousands of years he had slept there, but he didn't look dead. So the Bee alighted on Heiseb's right hand, and in order to wake him, so that he could ask for directions, the Bee stung Heiseb. And so it was, finally, after thousands of years, that Heiseb woke.

The Bee, after explaining that he was lost, asked Heiseb for directions, and Heiseb after plucking the stinger from his hand and returning it to the Bee, answered him. "Yes Bee," he said, "I will show you the way. But you must wait. Next dawn we will walk, you and I, but you must wait for me now because there is a thing I wanted to know. Rest here on my shoulder and we will start our journey tomorrow."

So the Bee took a spot on Heiseb's shoulder and waited. And when the day was over and the night had arrived, and the stars glittered in the dome above them, Heiseb pointed up at the stars and began to count. And hours passed as he counted each and every star, until finally, when he was done counting them all, he said to the Bee on his shoulder, "Nothing has changed. That is what I wanted to know."

Chapter 13

"What a wonderful story," Rebecca said.

"I'll tell you another tomorrow," John answered.

It was so satisfying to sit around a fire and listen to John's stories. She imagined how an African man must have told the same story to his children or friends five hundred years ago.

John was a carpenter in Cape Town. Sarah sold real estate. That was how they met, when a client had asked Sarah to find a reputable contractor and through various mouths had been told of John. This was about ten years ago. He was also involved in helping to build housing projects in an enormous township called Khayelitsha, he said, which was one of the neighborhoods that sprung up because of the pass laws.

"You can forget about what people earn per month, and education," John said. "The problem is that the bloody white regime didn't build a single home for the blacks in all those years. But they were very good at tearing down the shacks the people built for themselves. 45 years they were in power and they built nothing for the blacks. So now we've got a big problem isn't it? We've got more than twelve million blacks without proper homes."

"They've built five million homes in just ten years," Sarah added.

"That's right," John said. "Five million homes in the ten years I've been doing this. In a country of only thirty million people. Think about it, Becks..."

She was a little bit surprised, with his wife sitting next to him, that he gave her a nickname. She liked it but it gave her a vague feeling of discomfort.

"...I bet most of the people in your country wouldn't know how to build housing for forty percent of your population. But I reckon we've got seven million homes to go, 'cause it's not like a lack of water, housing, electricity, food or AIDS stops women from having more babies. That's the truth of the mother, isn't it? Reproduction? No matter what the situation, women will go on and on giving birth."

"It takes..." Rebecca started to say "two to tango," but Sarah was faster to comment.

"And now Mr. Potgieter is going to give all the women of the world yet another lecture on reproduction, as if everything was our fault." Sarah laughed as if she had heard this far too many times. "Oh, John, John, John," she said. She stood and paced away from the fire to face away from them. She lit a cigarette which she seemed to pull from the air. Until then Rebecca hadn't seen her smoke. Scott still stared quietly at the fire, ignoring what was going on, but when Rebecca looked over at John, he wasn't smiling. He was glaring at his wife's back.

"So now my wife's going to mock my opinions? And coming from her?"

Sarah didn't turn around.

"Is it?" John said.

Sarah took a long drag from her cigarette, and then a second one. Rebecca didn't understand the shorthand dialogue, but it seemed like they were having a fight.

Sarah turned and walked back to stand behind John. She held her cigarette between her lips and rubbed his shoulders. She spoke to him quietly. "I'm not mocking you love," she said and John's face softened. But there was something still there as he looked at the fire and let his wife rub his shoulders. Something still disturbed him. "It's frustrating," he finally said.

Rebecca thought he had the expression of someone who was staring at something he couldn't fix. Maybe it was South Africa and the problems of a relatively new government. He was a carpenter, so it must have been in his nature to fix things. Create them. She had sympathy for John, because she was a teacher, and her principal was forcing her to drop evolution because he was probably a secret religious extremist. It was her nature to try to expand minds, not format them; and perhaps it was John's to fix and build things, not see disease and poverty take it all down as soon as it was built.

Sarah rubbed John's shoulders a bit more, then patted him twice on the back with what Rebecca noted was some sort of condescension. It was not what she would have described as a loving pat but the type of touch that seemed to convey, "Get over it."

She decided his frustration was not about housing and poverty issues in South Africa but that something in his relationship with his wife. But John was presently back to talking about the difficult issues facing his country and was eventually back onto the touchy subject of race.

"If you hire an African man to dig hole," he said, "he'll show up with three others to help him. Each man will take a turn for ten minutes while the others watch. And then if you come along and say 'hey, look here, 'I'm not paying all four of you Oaks to dig a bloody hole,' they'll all walk off the job and pretend the hole's going to dig itself. And I'm telling you, you can have an Oak digging a hole for an entire year and you can check his work every day and every day it's perfect. But it's the one day you don't check it that he does it wrong. They are completely incapable of learning, and it's because of values. The white man values work and progress and thinks about the future and the black man isn't interested. And why should he be? He thinks why is it so important to dig this bloody hole? He'll just ask someone else for money whenever he needs it, and he'll get it too, because that's the way they are. You ask any of these men that work, even the hardest working ones, are they able to save some money or build up a nest egg for himself and his family? No. Because the minute he's got money in his pocket one of his lazy relatives comes along and says, 'Give it to me,' and he's got to do it, too, because that's the culture. If a friend or relative asks you for money you must give it to them. It doesn't matter than he just wants to gamble, you have to give it to him or you upset the family balance. And then later, when you ask him to repay, he must go and find someone else to give him some money so he can pay you back. And he'll do it too.

He'll always find the money to pay you back. But that's why none of them have any."

"So they're poor because they lend money to their friends?" Rebecca asked incredulously.

"No I'm not saying it's the *only* reason. I'm saying we're different. We don't understand each other. As races, we have different values and they're stronger than we are."

"Stronger? But you were just saying the white man plans for the future and the black man cares only about today."

"Doesn't it tell you something that he doesn't worry about the future? He's far more confident than we are. He has more faith in the world than we do."

"If you're, in fact, right, that he doesn't worry about it."

"You don't believe me?"

"I believe you believe it."

"So you don't believe me?"

"You haven't given me any evidence. And I find, in Ohio, that arguments about race or culture are almost always entirely devoid of real evidence."

John looked at Sarah for an explanation.

"You're on your own with this one love," she said, smiling, giving Rebecca a wink at the same time.

"It's always what one thinks," Rebecca continued, "but never what one knows. My best friend in the world is gay man and he keeps it quiet because we live in a small town and the people there have all these beliefs about homosexuals and what they are and do, and express their feelings bluntly, but they never have any evidence and if you ask them for evidence they get angry."

"And you think that's what I'm doing?" John said.

"I know it's what you're doing."

John looked at his wife a bit flabbergasted. Sarah was still smiling at Rebecca and Rebecca, maybe a little loose from the liquor, enjoyed the sense that she was getting the better of John.

"You're quite opinionated aren't you?" John said.

"No John," she laughed, then corrected herself. "Well yes I am. But I've also had too much to drink. But the fact remains that you gave me no evidence. You told me what your opinion is about the work ethic of the races but you gave no evidence. That's all I'm saying. It's what the whole world does. I'm a science teacher through and through. My mind doesn't really care about people's opinions."

"So you don't care about my opinion is what you're saying."

She laughed, because she knew the conversation was falling apart, probably due to the drinks they'd had, "I'm saying that I know what an opinion is and I never take it as a fact."

"What fact?" John asked, but this just made the two women laugh and had John staring at them with a befuddled grin. "What?" he asked.

Sarah stood and said, "I'm off to bed. Goodnight, Rebecca," and Scott dutifully jumped up to escort her back. "Goodnight love," she said to John and leaned over to give him a kiss on his head. Scott brought two more beers for John and

Rebecca before escorting Sarah back to their room. When it was just the two of them sitting around the fire, Rebecca sensed a shift and there suddenly felt, between them, a slight erotic tension, especially when John smiled, raised his beer to her and said, "Cheers." She caught a look in his eye. Or was it the smoke making his eyes water?

"But Becks, what I was trying to say," he said, much more quietly, and, even, intimately, "is that I decided when I was a very young man that I would never allow anyone to tell me what to do. That's why I could never go into the army or work for another man."

Is that what he was trying to say, she wondered? "But John what about traffic signals and simple rules about not cutting in line or stealing? We're told what to do all day long."

"Yes, but if I want to run a red light I will. If I want to steal something I will."

"So in other words you're an anti-social personality?"

"No, because I don't run red lights and I don't steal. I'm not interested in petty crimes. But I know, in the deepest part of my soul, that if I wanted or needed to do something, there isn't a man or woman on this planet that could stop me from doing it. They may make me suffer the consequences, but I believe we're not born to live like herd animals. There's only one person who I let tell me what to do and that's Sarah. But I'm a man and I wouldn't be able to live in this world if I didn't know that. I like being a man and I'll destroy myself before I let myself be feminized."

"But John, what makes you think anyone wants to feminize you?"

"It's the sense of things, isn't it? Men don't seem to have much of a place anymore. You women don't need us anymore."

"That's not true."

"What do women need us for, then? You just said your best friend is a poof. You obviously don't need a man or you'd be married, a beautiful woman like you."

She resisted the compliment (although she didn't want to), and said, "Julian is a man and I don't think you should call him a poof."

John nodded and said, "I mean... that's not what I meant. I meant that it used to be the case that women needed men and men knew their place in the woman's life. But now with everything manufactured and delivered right to your door, they don't need men to do anything for them except build some cupboards or fix the toilet. They don't even need the sex we give them."

He paused and the sense she had of him was that he was trying — almost ceaselessly — to create an understanding that would somehow set his compass right again. He looked up at her. A gust of smoke suddenly obscured him.

"Why don't you move your chair so you don't have to sit in the smoke?" she asked.

"That's probably a good idea," he laughed, "I've been sitting in this smoke all night, haven't I?" He stood and moved his chair not farther away from hers, but closer. He smiled at her and she smiled back, again, but she was aware that her pulse had quickened a little.

"You've got a beautiful smile," he said, "you look lovely when you smile."

"Thank you," she said. Yes, he was definitely hitting on her, but he was married and she wouldn't take that risk.

"You know, I've studied the people Rebecca. The Khoi people I mean. I've read about them. That's why I know all their stories. They used to be called the Hottentots, see, "Hottnots," but if you want to see a human being at his greatest... what I mean is this... oh Scott... "

Scott returned just then and didn't sit in his chair which was between John and Rebecca but took a chair that was on the opposite side of the smoke. Even though he wasn't between them, his presence created a chaperon effect. John looked at Rebecca when Scott took his seat and she guessed that he was disappointed. She felt disappointed herself, and it was hard to admit this. She understood John's wordless look and suddenly shared it, now that Scott was there making it impossible and thus, even more tempting. She knew that the temptation she was feeling and imagining now, if she stayed any longer, would easily overwhelm her senses and make her think that Sarah probably wouldn't mind it if they just quickly slipped off to her room. Plus Scott was sitting right there and had to walk them to their respective rooms, so they couldn't do that anyway, so she faked a yawn and excused herself and said she'd better be getting to bed since they had to get up so early. She said "Goodnight," to John who looked, again, surprised that she was leaving, and left with her escort feeling disappointed about the whole night.

Chapter 14

As Scott walked her back to her room, she heard low, snot-filled, snorts coming from underneath the walkway.

"What animals are those?" she asked.

"Those are the buffalo," Scott said. "Cape buffalo, not water buffalo. Everyone makes that mistake. They like to sleep under there. They sleep under the rooms too, so if you hear a sound beneath your floor, don't be frightened. It's just one of the buffalo."

They walked the rest of the way in silence. The moon had not yet risen, so it was dark, and the beam from Scott's flashlight swung back and forth ahead of them, in a bounce that kept pace with their footsteps on the walkway.

"Sleep well Rebecca," he said as he held her room's door for her.

She suddenly wondered how often Scott had been asked by guests to come in "for a nightcap." One of the perks of his job: sex with the horny tourists. Julian probably would ask him in. "You never know," he'd say.

She heard no buffalo sounds in her room so she assumed they weren't sleeping under the slats of her floor. "Cape buffalo, not water buffalo," she said, imitating and mocking her host, "Everyone makes that mistake... What an ass." *But how strange it would be*, she thought, *to sleep on a queen sized bed with a buffalo sleeping on the ground right underneath me.*

She stripped completely down to nothing and put on the white bathrobe that came with the room. She walked out to the veranda to look at the enormous field of southern stars in the great dark dome. She could see an influence of light just below the horizon which must have been the moon getting ready to show herself, like an old peeress preparing herself before entering a ballroom. It suddenly seemed tremendously mysterious, as if the moonrise had never happened before. She wished she were naked and was tempted to remove her robe.

She heard what she thought might be the same low and very distant *wuh wuh wuh* of the lion that they'd heard around the fire, but she couldn't tell for sure because it was so far away and faint. It was so dark.

If humans could see in the dark would we still have civilization, or language? Anything? She took a seat on the veranda thinking that she was going to enjoy the silence and watch the moon rise and forget all about John and the feelings she'd been having about him. Instead she felt a sudden dizziness that came from nowhere and passed just as quickly as it came.

"Oh please I hope I'm not getting sick," she said aloud and was suddenly startled when a whisper came from a few feet away, somewhere below her veranda off to the side. "Rebecca," he said. It was John. She jumped up from her chair and tried to see him, but it was still too dark still. She couldn't see a thing.

"John?"

He moved a bit closer so that she could see his face. As he came closer he emerged from the dark in an ethereal way — his round face becoming more visible as he neared the veranda.

He appeared to be floating, and wavered in and out of visibility.

"What are you doing down there?" she asked.

"I knocked on your door but you didn't answer."

"But what about the buffalo?"

"They're sleeping now," John answered.

"Well get up here where it's safe."

She wondered if he knew that she would invite him up because of the danger of letting him stay there on the ground. As he hoisted himself up she felt slightly pleased that he was pursuing her this way, but it was a little annoying too. What if she wasn't wearing the robe? He would have stood down there for God knows how long, staring up at her like she was a naked animal on display.

"I can't believe you walked down there."

"I knocked," he said again, as if it was some sort of excuse, "but you didn't answer."

"Of course I didn't answer, I'm out here."

"Enjoying the night air?'

"Yes. I was going to watch the moon rise."

"Can I join you?" he asked.

She stared at him for a moment and wondered if she should send him away. Of course she didn't want to. Opportunities like this were so rare anymore, and he fit the bill in so many ways. In her younger years she couldn't have cared less if some guy wanted to cheat on his wife, but she liked Sarah. She liked them both. They felt like they were her friends already.

"John," she said in that pleading, false way.

"John what?" he asked.

"You *know* what," she answered, but when he continued grinning at her, tilting his head slightly, she poked him in the rib cage and added, "Don't be bad." That tiny touch — the tip of her finger against his upper abdomen gave her a taste that made her turn her head and look away. The game. The game.

"No one's ever complained that I'm bad," he said, still grinning.

Oh men and their boasting, she thought. She instantly decided she'd had enough, but she couldn't make him leave the way he came in. Although the buffalo were, as he said, sleeping, she would never forgive herself if one of them woke up and attacked him. She decided to walk straight across the room to the front door so that he would understand he was supposed to leave. But it didn't work. He followed her into the room, stopped and glanced around.

"Your room's a bit different from ours."

"You'd better go John," she said, ineffectually holding the door open, "It's very late and it must be after midnight."

He was standing by the tea kettle and switched it on. He looked at Rebecca where she stood by the door. "Gorgeous," he said, and she found it hard to resist. She couldn't remember anyone ever calling her that. "Come over here," John continued, "Why are you standing by the door? I know you're not shy."

"Because you're married," she said. "What about Sarah?"

"I like women," John said.

"And?" she asked.

"So does she."

There was a moment before she actually registered what he said. "What?" she finally asked. She released the door and it slowly swung shut, making a slight catching sound as if they had been sealed in. "Are you... are you making that up?"

"Of course not. I'm not a liar."

"Well I'm... I'm surprised I guess but..."

"But what?"

"I don't know," she said, censoring herself. She was going to say that she didn't know anyone else who was in a similar position as she was. She and Julian weren't married of course, but they shared some form of love that was important to her. But here, now, was a man in the same position — the male version of herself; a heterosexual in love with a homosexual (*for that's what it was, wasn't it? Wasn't she simply in love with Julian?*) She suddenly felt a compatibility with John — or *comparability* might be a better word — which made her want to plunge into him, if it were possible. To swim in the sheets with him. To love the right type of man for a night.

"Does she mind if you...look outside?" she asked. "Does she look elsewhere too?"

"She loves me."

"What does that mean?" she asked.

"It means it is what it is. She likes you."

"So it's a gift?"

"Let's just say it's been a while."

"Does it upset her?"

John didn't answer, but merely stared at Rebecca until she crossed over to him and took the lead, kissing him with an intensity that might have shocked him at first, but to which he quickly caught up. They kissed until the electric tea kettle started to rumble and shake from the boiling water. He broke from her and shut off the kettle and the small lamp beside it.

"No one wants tea at this hour," he said.

She let him untie her robe and push it off her shoulders, unconcerned that she was nude and that he wasn't. She hugged him and kissed him again, finding it a strangely wonderful feeling to rub her naked body on him while he was still dressed in his shorts and oversized t-shirt. He sat down on the edge of the bed, pulled her toward him by her hips and used his fingers while she stood over him staring down. He stared up at her to see if she liked what he was doing. The moon had risen and had turned everything blue. His upturned face was blue. Her body was blue. She maneuvered herself into the bed while John quickly stripped. He wasn't wearing underwear, conveniently, and she was momentarily thrown by his readiness, or eagerness. But he smiled awkwardly and the brief moment of doubt disappeared.

It probably hadn't lasted as long as it seemed, but when he leaned his head down toward her and whispered, "Can I come inside," she nodded yes and prepared for the melancholy she always felt when, with a few ecstatic bursts, clenched eyes, perhaps a grunt or an 'oh oh oh' the male of her species finished his task and collapsed, as they all seemed to do, then fall suddenly into a coma as he rolled off of her, hit by a sudden loss of sugar or some other physiological thing she didn't understand. But John was different — she should have guessed he would be — and instead of falling asleep after his climax, he said, "Now your turn," and moved down, kissing her body until she was experiencing her own gasps and clutches. As he crawled back up to hold her and continue kissing her, she felt closer to him than she had felt to anyone in years.

Afterwards, the lion roared. She would have laughed at the cheesiness of it if it hadn't actually been happening. The lion must have come closer to the camp, because he was much louder. She found the call even more reassuring than when she had heard it around the fire pit.

"You hear that?" he asked.

"I'll never forget it," she answered, still panting, smiling.

"Did I tell the story about the lion and the virgin earlier?" She shook her head no, but he didn't elaborate. He began kissing her neck.

"I have to tell you," Rebecca said, "Sarah doesn't know what she's missing."

"I think she has an idea," John said, "We have sex now and then. Not often, but we do."

They were quiet and the world seemed quiet too.

~

"Fuck why am I lying? She doesn't like cock," John finally said, shattering the spell. "She doesn't like men, period. We haven't fucked in years. Six. Seven. I don't know anymore. Stopped counting. We love each other. Best friends. It's terrible. We had sex at the start but I could tell she didn't like it much. Made me feel like I was hurting her. And then she asked me not to. Said she couldn't change. And I promised I wouldn't."

~

"Did you know before you were married?" Rebecca asked.

"Yes," he said, "but what could I do? I thought she would change. I guess I could have tried to fall in love with someone else but it wasn't how I felt."

~

"Does Sarah look around?"

"She's got needs doesn't she? For all I know she's run off to Beatrice's room. But I hope not. I don't like that woman.

~

"I know why..." Rebecca said, leaving the thought unfinished. She almost spilled it. Should she? She felt John move his head to get a direct look at her.

"Why what?" he asked.

Cautiously she said, "I know why Beatrice was so upset."

"And why was Beatrice so upset?"

"Because she's never had an abortion."

"What do you mean?"

Rebecca sat up, scooted down to the end of the bed and placed her feet on the ground as if she was going to stand. But she didn't stand. She sat there, her hands gripping the edge of the bed and kept her back to John. She took a deep breath and held it, then started talking on the exhale.

"When I was leaving the clinic — the first time I mean — a group of protestors were screaming at me. They were sent there by St. Anne's, which is a local Catholic church, and they threw this red confetti on me — piles of it — because they couldn't be charged with assault since it was only confetti. At home later I was trying to get the paper out of my hair and I noticed that this confetti was actually little red paper fetuses. Some company or person built a machine to punch tiny c-shaped fetuses out of construction paper and package them and sell them so you can attack traumatized women. And when you're attacked that way you know what it is they really want to do. They don't want to paper you, they want to stone you. It's as old as the Bible.

"They're like Beatrice: all compassion for a baby impala but nothing for the hyena. And when she poisons them she will feel completely justified even though neither the hyena nor the impala have anything to do with her. I have this feeling these people are... Well I think it's because... Well you see, my father took me to have the first one and I didn't want to have it. That was the only one that I was forced to have."

"Becks," John interrupted, "how many abortions have you had?"

She looked up at the tent's ceiling before answering.

"Three." She waited for a moment before asking, still not looking at him. "Are you surprised?"

"A little. Haven't you heard of contraception?"

"Oh I could never have used contraception," she said, shaking her head.

He didn't respond and she took this as a sign that he was disgusted. She stopped speaking to him. She should have known he wouldn't understand, but she kept her back to him and looked out of the screen at the darkness.

"Becks?" John whispered.

"You don't need to worry John. I'm no longer able. The threat of pregnancy is over for me."

"Why are you mad?"

"You didn't exactly inquire about contraception a few moments ago."

"You asked me if I was surprised and I said, 'yes.' Why are you angry?"

"I may not be of much value to the world but I'm still convinced that I have something to contribute to it. The world won't be served by jailing me."

"Jailing you? What are you talking about? Becks," John said, "I don't understand why you're angry."

"Perhaps you'd better go."

"I'd rather not."

"Sarah will be waiting."

"Sarah will be sleeping."

She got up from the bed and crossed over to the writing desk. She picked her robe up off the floor and put it on again. She flipped on the water kettle and sat in the chair and stared at it. She was furious and disappointed, although starting to wonder if she wasn't just over-reacting because of how vulnerable she felt right now. She tried to speak in a normal voice. "I would really prefer it if you went back to your room."

"We're not allowed out of our tents. Remember? There might be lions walking through the camp."

"The threat of lions didn't stop you from coming here."

"Nothing could have stopped me from coming here."

She softened a bit when he said that. That mystical feeling of being wanted by another person — it always softened things. She was powerless against it. She reached out and took the teaspoon off the writing desk, which seemed to be there in order for her to do something.

"And for the record," John added, "I did ask and you said it was okay."

"Menopause," she said, "depressingly early." She turned her head to see his reaction, but he was only sitting up in bed smiling at her. His dark hairy chest made him look so masculine.

"Vasectomy," he said, making a small cutting movement with his fingers.

"Oh," she said, feeling utterly stupid. She looked back at the teaspoon and opened and closed the tin of Earl Gray.

"It's just that with our different needs, it was more important that we, or I rather, make certain that we avoid any complications that would... intrude, say... into our marriage. I didn't want to have a child with another woman."

A strange feeling came over her, just then, of a kind of loneliness. She and John both loved the wrong person for the right reasons; like so many. Love doesn't solve all problems. The kettle started to boil again, and it seemed to signal in its gurgling the end of this exchange. She couldn't even remember why she got so angry a moment ago.

She shut off the kettle and moved to the edge of the bed again, finding it easier to talk this way. She stared at the screen door that opened to her veranda, seeing nothing but the chair she was sitting in when John called to her from below. She could feel John staring at her back and she imagined his dark soft eyes ogling her, wondering at first, what she was talking about when she started talking about it again.

"I'm pretty certain I was sixteen the first time," she began, "and afterwards I told myself that the abortion was the right thing to do because the girls who didn't get abortions were taken out of school and put into an evening school. They were shamed one or another, and at least this way I could still take my advanced chemistry and biology classes.

"And it's not that I cared so much about school, because I had no great friends back then, but the first time he did it, you know, I really didn't know what he was doing. I used to wonder if I had been a more aggressive girl would anything have been different. But that's a question that's impossible to answer. I didn't know what to do because it was so shocking that you think that it couldn't have just happened. I thought to myself that maybe he was sleepwalking. That was the initial excuse I made for him and I held onto that excuse for a long time, because when my door opened and I said, 'Dad what is it?' I could see that he had a strange sleepwalking look. I don't know how to put it, but it was as if he had brought a curtain of steel down between himself and the world so that he didn't have to look at me. That was my first time, if you can call rape your first time. But since I never had a mother or an older woman — she died in a car accident shortly after I was born — I didn't know if it was normal to be frightened. He was my father and I wasn't supposed to be afraid of him. I was supposed to love him. And I did.

"So I did what everyone who's in an impossible situation thinks is the right thing to do, which was to do the wrong thing. I buried it and hoped that he never sleepwalked again. Except that he did. And again. And again.

"Then one morning I threw up in the kitchen, right at the breakfast table. He said, 'What's wrong?' and I said, 'Nothing,' but he knew. I knew too. I wasn't stupid. Every morning I tried not to be sick, but I was and then one day, before I went to catch the bus to school, he said, 'I've made an appointment for you at the clinic.' 'What clinic?' I asked. I pretended I didn't know what he meant. I wanted to ignore it, and hope that it went away. But he took me there and walked me inside with his arm over my shoulder. And all those people were there to scream at me, because the church sends them there and gives them bags of fetus confetti at their pot luck dinners. On the way in, my father got very angry with those people and he screamed, 'Go to hell you miserable fuckers! Leave us alone God damn you!'

"He had a huge deep voice and he was big so he was naturally intimidating. But they weren't impressed. A man kept trying to shove pictures of abortions in front of my face and a woman with a rosary walked beside us and shouted Hail Mary's in my ear.

"Once inside the clinic, I stopped crying and tried to compose myself for the check in procedure, and the talk with the social worker or whoever she was, who was there to make sure that this is what I wanted to do. My father filled out the form for me, or at least the single field he was worried about, which was the field for 'Father', or 'Male', it might have said.

"I know he wanted to make certain it said 'Unknown'. And when I was with the social worker by myself, she looked at the form and was obviously skeptical until I said, 'It was forced,' which was the truth. When she asked me if I wanted to report 'the boy' I said no and told her I was scared of him. And that was true too. But I wouldn't have told on him. By then instinct was my only guide and instinct told me to lie. And after that first time, I never cried about being pregnant or having an abortion again because... I don't know how to put it. I decided that to cry about the unfairness of life is to pity oneself and to hate the world. And I can't do that because... I..."

It dawned on her then. It came over her in a wave that she had never before understood what it was; why she had chosen earth science instead of history or English.

"Because I love life," she finally said. "I love life."

She paused for a moment and relished the thought.

"So I have a conflict about pity. Pity is like a reputation that you can't get rid of. Pity is a prison that other people build around you; a thing of their making. I can't be pitied. I can't allow it.

"But it continued, whether or not the anti-abortionists prayed for me or against me or pitied me or hated me. I could not have used contraception though. It would have made it seem normal. The only way I could cope was to think of it as a moment of evil that I had to bear. And in a way, a very bizarre way, I was lucky because most women say their molesters always say things like, 'You know you want it,' or 'I'm the only one who will love you like this,' or 'If you tell anyone I'll kill you.' At least he was silent.

"By the time I graduated high school I had come to accept that I wasn't going have the life girls are taught to dream about. So I decided I would become a school teacher. A local college was all my father said he could afford, although I think he probably wanted to keep me in the house, but that's why I ended up pregnant a second and third time, because I had to live with him while I went... oh... oh God!"

She doubled over as if she had been suddenly hit in the stomach, or needed to vomit, but she thrust her left hand behind her, to John, to indicate that he should stay away from her. Something about the pain of what she was finally confessing to this total stranger who she had just had sex with had suddenly enveloped her so completely she had to stop and... and stare it down. She knew she couldn't look at John or she'd never be able to finish, but John made absolutely no movement or sound. She slowly sat up again, wondered for a moment if he had fallen asleep, but she didn't want to stop to find out. She wanted to get it out.

"So I went to a local college and got a teaching degree and a job at a public school and then I finally was able to afford my own apartment and those horrible years were over. He said nothing when I told him that I was moving. But his look was... concerned... maybe even scared.

"Once I was on my own, I was twenty three, I just went hog wild, as they say, for a while. Like Julian. I made as many friends as I could. I had an IUD put in. I dated and slept with as many men as I possibly could. I'd drop them for the slightest of reasons like nose hair or blemishes. I was exercising my new found power, now that I wasn't under that man's roof. I thought I was catching up to all those things I had missed while my father held me captive.

"But I began to realize — slowly — it took decades to fully comprehend it — it's like a kind of dawning that takes the rest of your life and probably doesn't come fully into view until the very last moment when you go out of the world in a blaze of understanding — but I saw, eventually, that he enjoyed it. That it had turned him on and drew him toward me. My belief that he did it out of some sort of sick evil compulsion was just a hope that I maintained because I loved him. Of all things, I loved him. No one can understand that. Even I don't understand it.

"When I broke up with my last boyfriend — a sweet guy named Mark, I realized I had never loved Sweet Mark and that I probably hadn't loved anyone, ever. And there were no more men to try — they seemed to vanish overnight — and my girlfriends were married and having children and quickly forgetting me. Julian became my best friend. We met at a bar. We hit it off instantly. He's probably the first person I have truly come to love.

"And then I was forty four and I missed a period and then another and I realized it was the big M word. I was already menopausal. A single woman with nothing but abortions to her name. And it was so far in the past I hardly remembered it, but there I was, standing in my father's kitchen, having just returned from a visit to his oncologist.

"I had cooked him a couple of pork chops with a baked potato, and I was watching him butter his potato in this strange way he had. He was so peculiar about it. He would put the potato in a towel and then he would halve it. He would place the two steaming halves on a plate. Then he would cut three slits down the middle of each half, and he would then take a square pat of lightly salted butter and with his thumb and forefinger, shove a single pat into each slit, on it's corner so that it looked like a diamond. And he staggered them so that each half of the potato looked like the barbed tail of a dinosaur.

Then he would let the potato rest until the butter melted and left three yellow lines.

"And when he did this thing with the potato I said to him, 'Why did you do that?'

"He dropped his head and looked down at his lap, and thought for a very long time and when he finally spoke it was in a completely different voice: not his. He was looking at his lap — at his crotch — his weapon — and he said, 'I don't know.'

"I froze. I thought I would crack if I moved. Because I knew he was talking about those years when he came into my room, and his voice was the voice of that man that came into my room. And his entire explanation for happened was 'I don't know.'

"On the way home I thought about the two decades — more than two decades — that I had lived like this, all because of something he couldn't even explain. I didn't want to have to spend the night alone with those thoughts, so I stopped at the pharmacy store to buy a movie. I was looking for sort of nature program, when I spotted the cover of Meryl Streep and Robert Redford sitting in the grass in Africa. That was our movie. Julian and me, and we really were Streep and Redford in our own way. And I watched it again and then wanted, more than anything, to go away to some place like that, where the lions sit on your grave. Where I could be like that strong woman.

She paused.

"So I wanted to take this trip. And I don't feel guilty. I just feel that I *should* feel guilty. There are so many things we can't explain. So many things we do without understanding why, like all those animals. The world punishes women. And then it punishes us again. And once more after that. We've been punished enough and I've had it."

With that she was finished. She pushed her hands between her knees and sitting there in the dark, looked at the screen door opposite her. She wanted to turn around and look at John, to see what expression he had on his face, but she was afraid he would be asleep, having tired of listening to her. And if he was, well — it wouldn't really be much of a surprise would it?

But even so, please don't let John be asleep she thought. Just for once let there be someone who... she couldn't finish her thought: her little prayer to the Goddess if she inserted a Dear Athene at the start. *Dear Athene. Please favor me tonight, instead of someone else. Let my life be enough of a sacrifice. The carnivores always want more. Please let John understand me. Please let him be awake.*

Rebecca turned her head slowly. She almost jumped because John wasn't asleep. He was sitting up with one leg on the floor, staring at her with his mouth slightly slack, as if he was in shock. He was leaning forward with his arm resting on the knee of the leg that was tucked under the other. His look was so intense that it startled her, and she asked him, "What?"

Without saying a word, he stood in the very dim light and slowly walked around the bed to its end where she sat. Now because she was wearing the robe, he was naked and she was clothed. Feeling nervous she started to try to excuse herself by saying she knew she could talk a blue streak, but John lifted her from the bed and she rose willingly, knowing that he was going to embrace her, and he pulled her close to his naked body and hugged her, and she said, "John stop," but he didn't stop. And she said, "John please..." but he didn't stop. And then finally with the sundering of all resistance that she had built up over a couple of decades or more, she felt it burst into tears on his shoulder and she sobbed, because Athene heard her, and took tremendous pity on her, and sliced open her heart.

*

When her crying had run its course, John helped her back into bed. He removed her robe and helped her to lie down. He crawled in with her and pulled the duvet up to their chins. There were only about three hours to sleep before Bunte would be coming around with the drum to wake everyone up for the dawn drive, and Rebecca decided that she would skip it. Before they went to sleep, John told her another old Khoi story he had collected.

She listened to the ten thousand year old story drowsily, while she lay spooned into him, her head resting on his arm with the other wrapped around her body. She wanted to have sex again, and he was hard again so it would have been easy, but the feeling was more that she wanted to have sex as long as she could also sleep while it was happening.

"When Heiseb was a little boy," John said quietly, "he and his mother and father lived together in an area of the country which was dying. They were starving to death because the land was parched and had no more food. They were miserable, so

Heiseb's father said to his wife and son, 'Let us go and leave this land and search for food somewhere else.'

"After a while they came to a place where there were tall berry trees, full of ripe red fruit, and the trees were dropping their berries all over the ground where they could be picked up by anyone. And they were very happy. So they started to gather the berries off the ground to fill their stomachs. But the chief of the land was surveying his property and came by and saw what they were doing. So he rushed over and shook his fist and yelled 'Footsack' because, he said, 'these berries belong to me and my people.' And Heiseb's father said to the chief, 'But we are starving and we are as thin as twigs as you can see, and these berries are going to rot and go to waste.' And the Chief said to him, 'If I choose to feed the ground, who are you to tell me that I may not?'

"So Heiseb's father decided to demonstrate just how hungry he was by pretending to die. He said to the chief, 'Now because you would rather feed the ground, you have killed me. Look at what you have done.' And boom, the father fell down dead. His wife didn't know he was only pretending, so she began to wail, and she threw her head back and cried to the sky.

"After Heiseb and his mother had buried his father, they left and went to find food somewhere else. The next morning, Heiseb's father crept out of the ground, and began to the eat the berries. His wife had come to visit his grave and when she saw that he was alive, she wept with joy. 'You're alive,' she shouted, 'you're alive.' So his wife went running back to

Heiseb and she said, 'Your father is alive.' 'But that is not possible,' Heiseb answered, 'I saw him die with my own two eyes.' 'Come, Heiseb, come and see,' so Heiseb followed his mother to the grave and yes, indeed, she was right. There was Heiseb's father, walking around and eating berries. 'You see,' his mother said, 'your father is alive.' 'Yes,' Heiseb said, 'I see that my father is alive. Nevertheless, the dead must remain in the grave,' and he took out his machete and killed him."

Chapter 15

A few hours later she woke when Bunte came around beating the drum for everyone to wake up. John was still holding her. She could feel his warm breath on her neck and his morning erection pressing against her backside. She smiled because she had always wondered why it was "the morning" did that to men. But she had never asked anyone and never learned the reason, if anyone even knew.

She thought about last night and wondered what John would think when he woke. It certainly wasn't the way a normal night of sex ended, but out here — so far away from Illyria — so far away from her dead father, actually — somehow it had seemed like it was okay to talk about it. She wondered if she had flown halfway around the world just so she could tell someone.

She wanted to feel embarrassed but couldn't quite work herself up to it, but she felt different.

It also felt like something wasn't finished.

It was still very dark outside and the moon had set.

She was aware of a sense of being let down, too, as if she had thrown away something that had always given her strength. Her strength, *that she could stand it*, had been a false pride.

She maneuvered herself to face John which woke him. He opened one very sleepy eye and grinned. "Bunte's come around with the drum already," she said, "but I'm going to skip the drive this morning."

"That sounds like a good idea," John said and closed his eyes and snuggled closer to her. Then he opened his eyes, realizing. "Oh," he said, "I'd better get back to Sarah."

He sat up and swung his feet out of the bed. He shook his head and made a funny sound like a horse to wake himself up. He sniffed a few times, stretched his jaw. "My mouth hurts," he said, smiling and turning to look at her, "you wild thing."

"You're not trying to make me blush are you?"

"We had fun didn't we?"

"Yes," she said, "It was," and she paused before choosing the word, "memorable." She looked at him to try to say with only her eyes, 'I didn't mean to unload all that on you but I did and I'm not sorry.'

John said, after a moment, "I'm sorry for what happened to you Rebecca. I really am."

"It's alright John, it was a long time ago."

"So was apartheid," he said, "but the damage goes on and on doesn't it?"

She nodded.

John dressed quickly. He leaned over the bed and gave Rebecca another kiss, said they were leaving sometime that afternoon for their next camp so please, he said, try to be somewhere near the lounge for proper goodbyes and to exchange addresses. She said she would and he left.

Though it was still dark, there was a tiny suggestion of light creeping into the upper part of the sky. She fell back to sleep quickly, but at some point when the sun was up and had heated the room, she had a vivid and horrible dream of a doctor — a male doctor — pulling the head off of a cow which was lying on an operating table. The nightmare made her wake up with a gasp, and forced her to sit up in bed. Her heart was racing and her head hurt and she felt nauseated by the horrible dream.

She showered in her outdoor shower to clear the feeling. The water was delicious, wonderfully warm, and the soap they provided smelled of shea which was one of her favorite scents.

But another queasy feeling hit her in the stomach and upper abdomen, and then passed as quickly. It made her wonder again if she was getting sick. She remembered that she was due to take another Lariam pill tomorrow, but decided to take it a day early because this was the malaria season and she didn't want the her trip ruined before seeing the Carmine Bee Eaters. As she headed for the lounge she had, in the fresh air of the new day, a doubt about John and his relationship with his wife, so she was quite nervous as she walked along the long walkway. She imagined that Sarah would be waiting there and would attack her like a wife from some stupid talk show. But on the walk, nearly half a kilometer, she remembered the strange argument John and Sarah had around the fire last night when John said, "And coming from her?" And later when he said, "It's frustrating," while she rubbed his shoulders to soothe him. And then her condescending pats. She decided that John was telling the truth.

Just then she had a dizzy spell and stopped walking in order to steady herself on the rail. "Please don't get sick Rebecca," she said aloud, but a little half-heartedly because she was at that weak early denial stage where one knows it's happening but thinks it can be willed away. But this didn't feel like a cold or the flu or anything else she'd ever experienced, nor did it seem like something intestinal, and she hadn't had any problems in that regard.

She reached the lounge to discover the DeKoning family had not taken the morning drive either. A fatigued Marcel was asleep on his back on the long white couch at one end of the lounge, while Elizabeth and her two children were sitting in the central part. When the children saw her they tapped their mother excitedly. Elizabeth turned, waved and said, "Good morning Rebecca."

"Good morning Elizabeth," she answered and as she made her way over to them added, "Gut morgen Anton y Griet." She didn't know if that approximated Flemish or Dutch but it sounded close.

"You didn't go on the drive?" Elizabeth asked Rebecca.

"No," she smiled, "I didn't get much sleep. And you?"

"Oh..." was all Elizabeth said as she indicated Marcel with a kind of annoyed flutter of her hand. "The children would like to practice their English with you, if you wouldn't mind. They don't teach it in school until they're a little older."

"What are their ages?"

"Anton's six and Griet is four. Can I get you some coffee?"

Normally Rebecca would have said no thanks, and gotten it for herself, but she felt at ease and decided just to accept it.

"Yes thank you. Black please," she said and Elizabeth went over to get the coffee.

"So you'd like to ask me some questions in English?" she asked Anton and Griet, but they apparently needed their mother's presence or might not have understood her, and simply grinned at each other. Then they giggled and Griet buried her heads in the pillows of the couch they were sitting on. After Elizabeth returned and handed Rebecca her coffee, she sat on the couch and coaxed her giggling children into sitting positions, and told them something in Flemish which must have been a word or two of encouragement.

Griet spoke first, and her voice was soft and lovely and girlish. "Miss Over... where do you..."

She paused and looked at her mother, and her mother whispered, "li.."

"live in the... United... States of... America."

"Griet," Rebecca answered, "I live in a place called Illyria, Ohio."

Her mother translated and Griet smiled and plunged her head back into the pillow. It was Anton's turn then.

"What..."

"No, no Anton," Elizabeth said.

"Miss Over," Anton said and stopped. He was not as shy as his sister and instead of the embarrassed and giggling face his sister had, Anton's was strong and concentrated. He wanted to get it right.

"Miss Over," he said again, "do you live near McDonald's where you live... in the United States of America."

"There is one near me."

"What is it like where you live?' he asked.

"In the summer it's beautiful. It's very green and we have lots of trees and farms."

That was fairly true, Rebecca thought, as Elizabeth translated for her son. There were also empty factories, sections of terrible rural poverty, a shopping mall that was on the verge of extinction, a large strip mall that had been deserted for more than twenty five years and cavernous grocery stores with thirty registers but never more than three in use at any given time. The mall had put the downtown out of business, and then the giant box stores had put the mall out of business. Illyria was like a relic of different retail eras.

They passed the time quietly, Rebecca more or less taking Anton & Griet off Elizabeth's hands, who needed to return to her room. As Rebecca taught Anton & Griet the string games Cat's Cradle, Jacob's Ladder, Witch's Broom and the one where it looks like the string slides right through the fingers, every so often she looked over at the walkway where John and Sarah and the other guests would come in after their drive was over. She was feeling increasingly nervous about Sarah. Even if she had approved, as John had said, how could she *really* approve? But then did she disapprove of Julian's excursions to Cleveland? No.

Anyway, if she didn't want to upset Sarah she should have thought of that last night.

She heard the engine of one of the land rovers and tensed. She felt a knot form in the pit of her stomach, and took a deep breath to slow her rapid heartbeat. She looked back at Griet who was staring at her with an expression that startled her. Griet looked concerned, but not in a childlike, fretful way. It was too adult; too connected with her feelings. Griet reached out and took her hand and she was moved by this gesture, smiled at Griet and let her hold it.

Guests started to enter the lounge to get drinks before returning to their rooms to shower or change before lunch. Most of them she hadn't met. Carl came through, but without his married companions, so she was happy to see his dream vacation wasn't entirely ruined. He could continue on alone. But neither John nor Sarah showed up. Elizabeth had returned and had taken her children back from Rebecca so she decided to find Polly to ask her if she knew anything about the whereabouts of John and Sarah. She passed the sleeping Marcel on her way and because he was still on his back and his mouth was wide open she had a sudden urge to do a science experiment and drop a chocolate in his mouth to see if he started eating it in his sleep.

She found Polly at the other lounge, the lounge that was supposed to be for special guests, like royalty or movie stars or sports stars. Apparently a lot of them came to Botswana and asked for privacy. She asked Polly if she knew the whereabouts of John and Sarah Potgieter.

"Oh they've gone on to their next camp," Polly said, "they went straight from the drive to the air strip. Do you need me to send them a message? I can radio the camp. I think they were headed to Savuti."

"Oh no," Rebecca said too quickly, "I mean, was everything alright?"

"With the plane?"

"No. I mean, we had planned to have lunch together, but it's nothing."

"Yes, the planes operate on a very tight schedule. But because we had to send Beatrice and Alex away, changes had to be made in the schedule and planes had to be rerouted and so on. But don't worry, they'll have lunch at the next camp."

"Oh good. Thanks Polly," Rebecca said.

She returned to her room, sat on her couch and again, burst into tears.

*

The early evening drive was splendid, beautiful, gorgeous, dazzling, wondrous, splendiferous. But she missed John and Sarah the whole time. She felt like she had fallen in love with both of them. Then she felt stupid for feeling so. But there was something about the two of them that she wanted to keep. And now she would never see them again.

She was mostly quiet through dinner which was held, this time, at a different place — a place that was kind of a balcony that overlooked a flood plain full of water. When they heard animals trampling through the water someone turned on some flood lights to see what it was: it was a herd of female elephants, just passing by. They didn't mind the lights apparently — didn't even seem to notice them. They just walked. There was a child with them but it was nearly grown. She imagined it was the baby from the other camp, already mature and coming into her own. She imagined the family of females and their children were moving along with her on this trip, on foot, while she flew ahead to see them arrive.

And then they were gone and the lights were shut off and the candlelight dinner under the stars continued.

Life seemed awfully simple at that moment. Simple and mean.

Chapter 16

Nxamasere

The last camp on her itinerary was the most remote camp she was to visit and the one that she had specifically wanted because it had access to the Carmine Bee Eaters that lived in cliffs overlooking the Linyanti River. This was near a village called Shakawe. It was the deepest into the delta that she would journey; practically the farthest away from home that she could go besides booking a trip to the moon. It was also the most likely area for malaria because it was a water camp in close proximity to human habitation, and deep in the central malarial zone.

She took another Lariam pill when she woke before packing, thinking that like aspirin, two pills would be better than one. She still hadn't developed a cold and she had a bit more hope than yesterday that she had actually staved it off.

She'd had another nightmare though. This one was stranger, and harder to explain why it was so frightening. She had walked into her father's backyard and the entire yard was covered with tiny crosses — about six inches high — and all of them covered with sheer red veils. It was unnaturally terrifying but not for any reason she could understand. She pulled one of the veils off and screamed in her dream at the "horror" of it being uncovered. She woke up out of breath and discombobulated, not knowing where she was until she looked through her screen door at the landscape, and was reassured.

At Mombo's airstrip, while another gorgeous pilot was helping the DeKonings into the back of the Land Rover, it made her feel a bit more comfortable that the DeKonings had the same itinerary as she did. Even Marcel with all his bluster, demand for sweets and attention was becoming something like an irritating aunt that you get used to and find easy to dismiss: comfortable only because it's consistent and reliable and there.

The landscape changed as they flew farther up into the Okavango Delta. Instead of hundreds of little islands in a knee-deep sea, a single snaking river formed amidst a huge expanse of dark green papyrus. It was flat too; so flat in fact, that the river had almost no slope to guide it forward and snaked back and forth in large u-shaped bends.

The camp's manager, Nann, who was about Rebecca's age she suspected, had a deep manly voice, and she was a little bit disheveled. She was wearing two different socks, but she had beautiful smooth muscular legs and she was very tan. Like Rebecca she had long hair in a pony tail and for a moment, Rebecca fancied that Nann was her doppelgänger; a woman who lived as she might have, had she been lucky. They drove for about ten minutes to a wooded area where they were to board a boat. She explained to Rebecca (because the DeKoonings had been here before) that, "up here at Nxamasere the water's permanent, so all the flora and fauna adjust to the fluctuations in the river's height. But it never dries out up here so you'll see some lechwe and crocodiles but no other animals. Maybe a Jumbo."

"A Jumbo?"

"An Ellie. Elephant. Oh and we've got a young hippo in the channel too. I'll tell you about him in a bit. But we've got some of the most beautiful birds in all of Africa here and a Fish Eagle we call Jeffrey — we'll get him to show you his fishing skills and you can do some fishing of your own if you want. That's mainly what we are; a fishing camp."

Rebecca didn't want to ask just yet if they would have a chance to see the Bee Eaters. Once they were settled she would inquire. She'd be crushed if they couldn't: to have come so close but not be able to see them.

When they arrived at the spot where they were to catch their boat, Rebecca looked up in the trees and saw monkeys scrambling through the branches, while other monkeys stared down at the tourists with huge dark eyes.

"You didn't say you had monkeys here."

"Oh Christ I wish we didn't. They're Vervet Monkeys and I'd shoot every one of them if I could."

"What?"

"They're so cheeky, you have no idea. They steal things. Horrible bastards. I once saw one climb in over the wall of the lounge and he didn't see me. So I let him come down and he picked up the creamer for the tea and coffee and started to drink it and I had a towel in my hand and I gave him such a whack." She roared with laughter at this memory. "Oh he jumped nearly all the way to the ceiling and ran out so quickly.

Dropped the creamer but I didn't mind at that point. It was worth it. I had such a good laugh. Stupid little thieves."

While Nann helped her assistant load bags onto the boat, Rebecca stared up at a monkey who held a twig in its hand and was staring back down at her. (It was so odd to hear everyone describe animals with human failings — theft, murder, laziness, stupidity, sneakiness. They weren't really any of those things were they? Could they be?) The monkey and Rebecca looked at each other for a few moments and then the monkey made a little screech, dropped the stick and scampered away. She didn't sense anything had passed between them in the way that a dog or a cat can look at you and some sort of species-to-species communication happens, wordlessly.

After they finished loading their bags onto the boat, which would take them to the small island just on the other side of the channel, Nann said, "Right. Now we'll take the boat the rest of the way and you can unpack and rest for a bit before tea and our sundowner. Then you'll get to meet the other guests. We have two other couples with us and I'll introduce you later. But I'm going to have to ask you to be discreet please. It's a little awkward but we'll all manage."

Rebecca wanted to ask what she was talking about. Discreet? What did that mean? Something clandestine?

"Right," Nann said as they began boating to the island, "I'll give you a bit about the one rule of the camp. The one rule is there are no rules. You can walk anywhere you like and you can walk yourselves to your room and carry your own torches. We're not like the other camps. A little more down to earth here. The only thing I must ask you to remember is that we have a little two ton fellow in our channel. He's a hippo we've named William. At night he sometimes comes up the banks and onto the island. If you see him, just turn around and walk back to your room and shout for Adam. If you're coming from the lounge, then turn around, come back to the lounge and one of us will chase him away. He hasn't hurt anyone but as I'm sure you have heard hippos are very dangerous and we don't want anyone getting mauled. He may be a youngster but his tusks are already ten inches long. Well here we are."

The boats pulled up to a dock and the usual open aired arrangement of lounge, bar, dining table and fire pit. The camp was not nearly as fancy or luxurious as the previous two. The second to fifth guests rooms were built off a plank walkway that ran down the center length of the small island. The walkway was not raised like it had been at Mombo. It was simply there so guests didn't have to walk on the ground. The first guest room was at the opposite end of the island, on the other side of the lounge and dining area. It had its own walkway and was distinctly separate from the rest.

The rooms here were solid, built of concrete on three of the sides. The fourth wall was just a low wall, about mid thigh high, also made of concrete. Each open aired room faced the river like a small private stage. The missing wall was covered by a heavy white curtain which, when drawn back, revealed a bright chalk colored room with a large mahogany bed under a mosquito net; a chair, a writing desk, and a bathroom behind it. Between the first guest room and the other four was the dining room, lounge, bar and fire pit, all open to the channel.

When tea time came, after a short nap that didn't really make her feel better — she walked to the lounge and met one of the other couples: Gerard and Sandy Miller, from Scotland. But she didn't notice anything about them that required the discretion Nann spoke of. They exchanged some difficult small talk until the DeKonings arrived and the conversation became a little bit easier because Marcel was so reliable in talking about himself.

She made some tea then, and she stood a bit away from the others. The children were playing quietly with a board game while Elizabeth and Marcel spoke to Gerard and Sandy. She felt a little bit alone. She wished, for the first time on this trip, that Julian was with her.

She thought about John again and smiled, thinking about the fun they had. She regretted not getting his number, or their number, rather. His name was Potgeiter. She decided to write it down so as not to forget and maybe find him later.

She saw some books on a shelf, took one, sat down at the chair that was farthest from the bar and pretended to read it. It was a book about the Okavango fish but only about the fish, not about the more interesting question, to her anyway, of how fish came to exist in a desert. The source of the water was the mountains in Angola — the other end disappeared in sand, just beyond the town of Maun. She imagined what she would have to say in the future if a student ever asked such a question.

"That's just how our glorious and everlasting Intelligent Designer designed it," she would say.

Nann emerged from the back, interrupting her fantasy, took stock of things and said, "Right. Has everyone got tea? Yes yes. I guess we're just waiting for Donna and Bill and then we'll be off after they have some tea. We can use one boat and I think we'll take a ride up the Okavango to see Jeffrey. And of course we'll have a look at Kingfisher Cove. How 'bout you Rebecca. Have you got tea?"

"Yes," Rebecca said. Nann's eyes suddenly shifted to look behind Rebecca. She said, "There they are. Hello you two. Donna. Bill."

The last two guests had arrived at the lounge from the other direction where the first cabin had been built with its own walkway. Rebecca turned to look and blanched when she saw them, as Nann went around pointing fingers and introducing them to the new arrivals. "Donna, Bill. This is Rebecca, from America, Gerard and Sandy, from England, and the DeKoning family, from Belgium, and I think I've got the names, it's Marcel, Elizabeth, and the children are Anton and Greta."

"Griet," Marcel interjected and eagerly moved forward to meet the new couple.

Donna reached forward before greeting Marcel and shook Rebecca's hand, and then moved over to the bar to greet the others, as did her companion Bill. Rebecca was too stupidly flustered to stand but Donna gave no indication to anyone with either a wink or a nod to indicate "Yes, it is I."

She was a world famous actress. Some said she was the most beautiful woman in the world. And she was extraordinarily beautiful in person.

Rebecca looked at Nann behind the bar, to try to get some confirmation of what she believed, but Nann was only tending to some paperwork, making small tick marks for someone's drink tab. A look at the other guests, however, confirmed that they all knew it. They all had the same wide-eyed and happy expression as she must have had at that moment. And they all looked like they were trying not to have that awed, happy look. She was apparently staying in the camp under an assumed name, and she was here! Staying in this camp! A famous person! And she had just met her! A famous and beautiful actress had just emerged here from wherever they live, to be among them for awhile, and be just like them.

She had never seen a famous person in real life. The idea of fame all came through the television screens or the movie screens. It was only because of the screen that the stars were real. Cathode saints, she thought. Human but slightly larger than human, with followers.

And this one was thought to be so beautiful that it wouldn't have mattered when she lived. She would always have been fated to be this creature of beauty. But here she was, anyway, and it was very exciting to think they were going to spend two days together and maybe get to know each other. Her mood lifted and Rebecca suspected the excitement was with all of them.

After the greetings, "Donna and Bill" moved away from the group and had a seat in one of the chairs which faced the Nxamasere channel. Bill brought her a cup of tea with some shortbread and had a seat in the chair next to hers. The two sat, facing away, wordlessly. They periodically nibbled at the shortbread or sipped their tea, but otherwise the two seemed still and frozen as they looked out across the channel and its backdrop of papyrus. It looked as though all the images of her had taken over her real life, looking less alive and increasingly like a statue.

Having calmed from this initial brush with fame, Rebecca sat on the couch in the lounge area and flipped casually through the book about fish, as if she was actually interested in the fish. This was the worst part of traveling alone, as she knew it would be — the awkward times when there were only couples around her.

Why on earth was she so suddenly in a bad mood?

Nann came out from behind the bar. Leaving the other couples to entertain themselves, she walked over to the lounge area and had a seat with Rebecca. "So howzit Rebecca? Are you alright darling?" she asked.

"Yes," Rebecca answered, cheering a bit when Nann called her darling. She dropped her voice to a whisper, "Is that who I think it is?"

Nann spoke lowly, "The booking says her name is Donna. Bill and Donna Hedges."

"But she looks exactly like her. With her beautiful blue eyes? And Bill looks like her husband. And he's shorter than she is?"

"I know. But they say they're not, so that's what we have to assume."

"But is that what you think Nann?"

Nann smiled, but didn't answer for a moment. Finally she said, "Let's just say I'm not at liberty to say. If she says her name's Donna, then that's who she is to me. You've told me your name's Rebecca, so why should I think it isn't? Anyway what's the difference between a person and a name and a person and a fake name?"

"The name," Rebecca said, laughing.

Rebecca smiled. "True," she said. "Prince Harry's been here twice you know. But for him we empty the whole camp."

"Nann, I was wondering if we'll be able to have a chance to see The Bee Eaters birds in their cliffs? They're supposed to be near here. At least that's what I've read, that this camp was the closest."

"Up by Shakawe?"

"Yes, I think so."

"Sure I think we could do that. I think the others would like that too. It'll take all day because it's quite a long ride, but we can do that tomorrow. Wonderful idea."

*

Meandering up the river that evening was peaceful. They were all in one large flat bottomed boat sitting in director's chairs. Rebecca sat in the front row with the children. The famous actress was in the back of the boat with her husband and the others were in the middle. She felt, oddly, split off from the adults by the two youngsters, but she found youngsters could be very comforting sometimes and she was enjoying having something to do, when she would direct Anton and Griet's attention to a beautiful bird on the bank of the river. She was teaching again. It was so natural to her.

It was still sunny and a bit on the warm side, but she could feel an occasional cool draft come up from the river. Nann had told them all to get their "jerseys" so she had a jacket curled up in her lap. She had forgotten her camera again. Ridiculously, she had yet to take a single picture.

The driver of the boat was a fellow named System and he drove slowly so that he could spot birds and crocodiles. The first crocodile they saw was about four feet long and slipped quickly into the water as soon as he pointed it out. Rebecca had only seen it for a couple of seconds but she was gripped by a paranoid feeling that it was coming toward the boat to get her. She looked forward, away from the spot where the crocodile had been resting, and calmed herself by putting her hand on her heart.

She preferred the birds.

There were so many of them; she didn't even attempt to remember their names but just stared and tried to keep the images in her mind. Large beautiful black birds with shiny wings and long slender necks. And then clutching to a reed here and there were tiny blue, red, and orange Malachite Kingfishers, no bigger than the palm of her hand.

The purpose of this excursion was to meet Jeffrey, the Fish Eagle. At some rather large pond-like section of the river, near a grove of trees, System stopped the boat and Nann started skewering some raw fish meat with skewers of papyrus, while Marcel began setting up his enormous camera and tripod. Jeffrey was an African Fish Eagle which had become comfortable enough to "perform" for the tourists. Nann pointed up to where Jeffrey was perched at the top of one of the trees. He looked exactly like an American bald eagle, but smaller. When they were almost ready, Nann started calling, "Jeffrey! Jeffrey!"

Yes there was a distinct reaction, Rebecca noticed. He turned his head a little. He knew the name he had been given. He wasn't going by a fake name. Names. An animal can know its name. How is that possible?

Nann explained to those with cameras how to prepare to photograph Jeffrey, then threw one of the big chunks of fish meat in the water, which floated because of the papyrus. Rebecca looked up at Jeffrey in the tree and he did nothing for about a minute while Nann called his name. Then he lifted up his wings and soared. He made a graceful right turn toward them, not even flapping a wing but maybe a single time. Nann said, "Start shooting now," and the cameras on board all went off at once making a huge twicking racket, as Jeffrey swooped down, extended his claws in front of his body, expertly grabbed the fish bait in his claws and took off again, quickly pulling his legs behind him and making another graceful arc back to the same tree in which he had been sitting.

Of course she forgot her camera and would not be able to show anyone back home pictures of this, but it was enough to see it.

On the way back to the camp they stopped at what Nann called "Kingfisher Cove." It was just a very narrow channel that appeared to dead-end in a bunch of Papyrus reeds, except there was something special about this dead end in that it made a lovely little cove. And inside — they needed to use flashlights because it had gotten too dark to see — if you carefully parted these reeds, were twenty or thirty tiny Malachite Kingfishers, all sleeping. Twenty or thirty tiny birds: red beaks and feet, crimson chest, bright blue backs. They used this natural cove as a protective home. Snakes and other dangerous creatures couldn't get to them here. The lights disturbed them a little bit, but they didn't fly away or do much of anything other than move their heads a little. Some of them didn't even wake. It was so peaceful. They looked like ornaments on a tree and everyone fired their cameras like the paparazzi that usually pestered the famous woman sitting in the back of the boat.

*

Before dinner, in her room, she was feeling put out again by the fact that everyone was partnered. Nann was doing what she could do to keep her involved, but Nann had other jobs to do and had to take care of the other guests too.

At dinner she was seated next to Nann just as she was seated next to Scott at Mombo. "I guess this is the single person's chair," she said, making a joke no one understood. Across from her sat the star and her husband, a country western singer. She, the star, had said little on the boat but in what she had said, Rebecca recognized the same alto voice. There was something very annoying about being forced to pretend that she wasn't who she was and Rebecca, getting more annoyed by the minute, was only able to keep it to herself through the appetizer course, which was butternut squash soup. Just after they served the roasted lamb which, like every meal, looked absolutely delicious, Rebecca finally had to ask, discretion be damned.

"Excuse me," she said, "but I just have to ask. I don't know if anyone has already asked you this question, but aren't you Nicole Kidman?"

She could feel Nann, to her right, tense up at this breach of protocol. Donna smiled at first and looked down at her plate, as others looked on, eager, probably, for the affirmation but unwilling to break the code of silence. "No," Donna said, smiling, "I'm not."

"Well the resemblance is amazing," Gerard said.

"I know... I get it often. But I'm not her."

"Because you look exactly like her," Rebecca continued, "Exactly like her. Your hair. Your cheekbones. The color of your eyes. And you even have the same voice. You have the same Australian accent."

"So do twenty million other people."

"But they don't look like you," Rebecca said.

"No. And they don't look like her either. My name's Donna," Donna replied.

Rebecca nodded and looked down at her plate. She wasn't feeling hungry anymore, though it would be sad to miss this meal. She found herself even more irritated by the attitude of this actress, by the attitude that here in this camp, that they couldn't all just sit down together, unmasked so to speak, and talk like normal people. Except it wasn't Donna's fault; it was her own. She wanted Donna to be like herself; she was feeling so exposed.

Telling John the truth made her feel vulnerable to everything in the world, while across from her sat this beautiful woman, a stunningly beautiful woman, who wasn't vulnerable to anything because she could just sit there and smile and pretend to be someone else.

People, especially men but both sexes, would trip over their own feet to be able to do something for her and to be near her and to feel the presence of her.

But who did she think she was anyway? Only Nicole Kidman would have the nerve to pretend she was someone named Donna, so obviously this woman was, in fact, Nicole Kidman. There's the proof, Rebecca thought, right there in the folds of my argument. But then she realized that it was probably best just to go to bed. It would only make her angry to have to sit there and make small talk with Nicole Kidman and pretend she was someone named Donna.

But what if she *was* someone named Donna?

What in the hell was wrong with me anyway? Rebecca thought. She was having so many mixed feelings. This couldn't be menopause. She should, by most accounts she'd read, be coming to the end of menopause.

"You know Nann," Rebecca said, "I'm not feeling well. I think I'd better go to bed."

"Tell me what's wrong?" Nann said with a surprising urgency in her voice.

"I'm not sure," she said, "I don't really have much of an appetite and I feel queasy. But I've been feeling kind of ill all day. For a couple of days actually."

"Alright then, just grab a torch...oh wait a minute," Nann said. "You're not taking Lariam are you?"

"Lariam? What?"

"For Malaria."

"Oh. Yes I think so."

"Oh shit. Well stop then. Don't take another pill. You have absolutely no idea how many vacations are ruined by that medicine. When did you take the last one?"

"This morning."

"Aggh shit. Okay well then, we'll see how you are tomorrow. Some people have no problems, some feel sick for a day but have no more trouble after that. But with other people, their hair falls out or they start vomiting or they get frightened and they hallucinate and lose their minds. They think everyone's looking at them. We've even had to evacuate some people out. They won't come out of their rooms and we have to drag them out."

Hearing these side effects made her feel as though her stomach had fallen out of her body. She suddenly felt that she was far away from things, and very vulnerable. Evacuation! Such a dangerous sounding word. It all seemed suddenly precarious, one's health. She was suddenly aware that she could die out here. That she could die anywhere! "I don't want to be evacuated," she said, too panicked. "I came all this way to see the Carmine Bee Eaters, I don't want to be evacuated."

"No worries. No worries Rebecca," Nann said, calming her, "it's probably just a 24 hour reaction. The problem is that the American doctors prescribe this garbage and all you yanks take it for a couple weeks before you come here, then while you're out here you go bonkers, eh? But by the time you get back to America you've stopped taking the pills, all your symptoms disappear, your md's don't find out what the medicine they prescribe is doing, and they're too lazy to find out and they don't listen to anyone over here, of course, and so in the end everyone thinks that Africa's just a lousy stinking place full of poverty. But it's the medicine, I'm telling you. Shoo. Some of those shootings in the military are caused by Lariam. When you get home, do me a huge favor, please, and tell your doctor. I'm so tired of explaining about what Lariam does to people. You're much better off taking your chances with the mozzies. The pills don't always work anyway, and yes, we're near Nxamasere village, but there's no malaria there so you're really not likely to get it. But one thing I've learned. Americans can't spend enough money on drugs."

"Well I won't take it anymore. I haven't been bitten too badly anyway. Just a few bites on my ankles."

"Well we'll still try tomorrow to go and see the Bee Eaters if you're game and feeling up to it. Alright darling? We'll see how you are tomorrow. We'll go in the afternoon. Plus I've arranged a surprise which I think you'll like, so that'll be a reason to stay well. Decide in the morning. If you're really not feeling well then I think you should sleep late. Adam will bring you coffee in the morning, around seven. We'll just make sure it doesn't get worse. And here's what... if you have to go back to Maun, I'll go with you."

"Oh thank you, Nann," Rebecca said as she stood, feeling grateful and wanting to cry. Goodnights were exchanged with everyone, including Donna with her lovely trained voice. "Goodnight Rebecca," she said, and Rebecca answered, "Goodnight Donna," without betraying her doubt of the name.

"Night Rebecca," Nann said, "If you see Willie on the way to your room, just remember to come back here and we'll have Adam go out and chase him away. We love him, but he's still a wild animal, so you must shine your torch ahead of you and if you see him, don't try to pet him or talk to him or do any other foolish things, alright? Just back away slowly and return to the lodge."

"I won't," Rebecca said, and she left after saying good night to the DeKoonings and Millers. The children got up from their chairs to kiss her goodnight — European style — and she was touched. She walked down the wooden boardwalk and waved the flashlight back and forth ahead of her. It was very dark here, thick with trees. It didn't seem likely that a hippo could come up here, so she wasn't concerned. Suddenly, a thousand tiny whistles started all around her: tiny single notes. It frightened her so she hurried back to the dining area. Nann looked at her when she emerged from the dark path.

"Did you forget something Rebecca?"

"No, but I heard people whistling."

"Oh no no," she laughed, "I was just explaining to the others. Those are the Reed frogs. Tiny little things but they make a huge noise don't they? That all start at the same time and then they all stop at the same time. You can practically tell the time by them."

Rebecca smiled and turned to go back to her room. The sound of their whistles surrounded her, but seemed more concentrated to her left, near the water of the channel. For a moment, in a sudden flush of paranoia, she felt that the frogs were tiny people whistling at her — a kind of ululating — as she traveled this wooden path and swished the light of her torch ahead of her, in arcs, to make sure she didn't bump into the giant beast: the riverine horse called William.

Nann had told her to take the torch and frighten away one of the most dangerous beasts in Africa, William, the young hippo: citizen of rivers, alien of land, territorial, violent, killer of its own children. The poor boys grow up alone, Nann had said, because the fathers try to kill the boys, their sons, and the boys must run away and find their own water space, until they're old enough to return to the source of all their troubles and kill their fathers. Then they do the same to the next generation.

Nausea gripped her stomach as she thought about William the Hippo and the violence of that life. She held onto the railing of the tiny boardwalk, and when the nausea passed and her stomach relaxed, she finished the walk to her room. Her bed was turned down but the lights were off, so as not to attract bugs in the open-aired room. She left all the lights off, undressed in the dark to her underwear and bra, slipped underneath the mosquito net and sat cross legged on top of her bed, staring at the world through the missing fourth wall. It was so dark now, but not quiet at all, because of the frogs, calling each other for sex. The dark mysterious sex that she used to feel had been the source of great pain, until that era had passed and she had learned to revel in it — or supposed she had reveled in it. She had a new, distinct feeling now that her sex life had been reactionary; that everything in her life had been a reaction to him, that man; not getting married, going to community college, keeping all men at a certain distance, becoming a school teacher, getting close to Julian, then taking care of her father in his final dotage, illness and death. This might be the first time in her life when she was not simply reacting.

She breathed deeply and smelled the air, which was moist here, and she could see that the moon was emerging from behind some clouds. As the landscape, the papyrus and the channel began to take form again and she could see the silver light on the barely rippling water. She felt as if she was completely outdoors in her bed, under a gossamer canopy, and she closed her eyes and imagined that instead of one missing wall, there were four missing walls of this room — and that she was lying on her bed in the bright sunlight in a large field, visible to everything and everyone.

People concealed themselves in hides or behind trees and bushes and false names so as not to startle her or intrude upon her routine. She lay there on this bed in this open field with all her sins revealed, apparent to all the amateur paparazzi of Illyria, who stared at her with binoculars and took pictures of her with large gossipy lenses, like Marcel's. And she imagined that everyone who saw her, rather than wanting to punish her or control her, tried to understand her, as if they were travelers from another time and were only here to investigate the adult behavior of the human female victim of teenage incestuous rape.

There was a crack and Rebecca opened her eyes, interrupting her meditation. She was certain she heard a very loud split — a large branch being stepped upon by a heavy animal. It was the sound of an animal stepping on a branch, she was sure, right outside her wall-less room. She panicked, but only slightly, because the small half wall was enough of a barrier that William the hippo wouldn't cross it unless he was angry. But she had left the little door open. She took her flashlight in hand and quietly moved out from under the mosquito net. She reached over and pushed the small door closed and then she turned on the light and shined it out of her room.

She swept the light back and forth, expecting to see the hippo. But the only thing she saw were the trunks of thick trees and dead leaves, and dirt and twigs and matted grass that led down to the water of the channel about fifteen feet away. She felt foolish, but she whispered to him anyway. "William? Hippo? Hello? Hippo? Are you there?"

She listened but heard no more cracks or walking noises — just the continual whistles of the frogs. Occasionally she heard the muted group laugh of the guests from whom she felt somewhat alienated. They were eating the main course now, she supposed. Perhaps in their bonding, Donna had finally admitted to everyone that she was, in fact, Nicole Kidman, and that the entire world knew her face and name and that she had won many awards, including an Oscar for her triumphant portrayal of Virginia Woolf.

She could see nothing that could account for the crackling sound she heard, so Rebecca switched off her flashlight, drew the room's heavy curtain closed, crawled back under her mosquito net, under the covers and into bed. She felt fine, without nausea anymore, and she hoped that tomorrow she would be able to go fishing with the other couples. As she lay there, she thought of the tiny Malachite Kingfishers, sleeping in their little cove of papyrus reeds, safe from snakes and the larger birds. She wondered if they could wonder at themselves, the way she wondered about herself and other people in her life. They were so amazing.

Before me, the universe, she thought, and that would have been her last thought before falling asleep that night, except that out of nowhere she remembered a television clown asking a veterinarian on some sort of dumb show, if he had any hippototamisses to see. And that was how Rebecca fell asleep that night, with a clown standing over her and repeating over and over, annoyingly, "Where's your Hippo-Totamiss Miss? Miss? Where's your Hippo-Totamiss? Miss? Miss?"

Chapter 17

Rebecca woke the following morning with the distinct feeling that she was no better. But she was in no way going to spend all her money, come all the way over to this continent, and give up on her goal to see the Bee Eaters. She decided that she was going to fake being well.

The feeling was no longer one of physical queasiness. It was more of a feeling of unease or dread. It had moved from her stomach to her head. She felt scared, as though she knew something terrible was going to happen today, and the room with the heavy white curtain as its fourth wall only added to the low grade paranoia. Though it was still quite dark in her room, someone had placed a tray with coffee and biscuits on the table next to her bed. From behind her mosquito netting she stared at it and had the urge to scream. She wondered if it was a man who had pulled back the large curtain to place it there. Had he stared at her for a minute or two? Had he licked his lips and contemplated raping her? How long had her father stared at her? How long — how many years — had he suppressed it, or did the idea only come to him that night? Does the man who does that suddenly think, "Oh ho hee hee hay hay, I'm going to rape my daughter to-day," No. Never. It had been there for awhile. For the first time in her life she hated her mother for not being there to protect her. Rebecca had always kept thoughts of her mother in a safe place, emotionally. When she was young she used to imagine all her kindness and motherliness based on a few old photographs of her mother holding her young newborn.

But today she was mad at her.

"Stop it," she said aloud.

Had she survived the accident she might not have been able to protect her anyway. That kind of thing can happen right under a mother's nose and she, the mother, for whatever reason, doesn't know what to do about it. How do you battle something like that? First of all, just to believe the possibility it takes such an extraordinary leap of the imagination; of the mind.

Someone whispered inside Rebecca's head: *Nobody knew. Nobody knows. Nobody is a somebody who wants you to pay.*

She shook her head to clear away these jumbled thoughts, which seemed to come from somewhere else — some judgmental voice. She lifted the mosquito net to get out of bed. *Funny,* she thought, as she walked to the bathroom, *the effect of the mosquito on human history, but also the horse, the dog, the temple cat, the bed bug, the louse. My kingdom for a horse. A horse. A horse. What a magnificent description of the human struggle.* Then she got lost, suddenly, sitting there on the toilet, in a non-thought for a few seconds — a blank that held her attention as sharply as an interesting fact about geology.

These random racing thoughts and blanks continued as she showered, dressed and prepared to meet the DeKonings again and the star named Donna, and the other people whose names she had forgotten, until it came time to open the curtains on her missing fourth wall. Except that she had a sudden fear that

William the hippotatamus would be standing there, ready to attack and kill her, like an audience waiting to pummel an actor with tomatoes.

"He's not there Rebecca," she said aloud, "pull yourself together."

But she was suddenly more frightened than frightened and every time she reached for the curtain, she pulled her hand away before touching it. Finally, in the way children ease themselves into cold water, she opened it a fraction and peered out through the crack of light, then opened it some more until it was fully open and the great day was completely there: brown leaf littered earth, green flora, the huge blue sky, and no hippo.

She was surprised when she arrived at the lounge and dining area to discover that she was the first guest up, not having realized that it was still early. She sat in the chair that Donna... (remember to say Donna she told herself)... had used last night and looked at the river and at the thick tall Papyrus reeds that choked the shore on the other side of the narrow channel. It all looked so ancient somehow. It seemed like she was living a thousand years ago; that she had traveled through time and she was Cleopatra, sitting beside the Nile, waiting for the asp, because she had sided with the wrong man. Wasn't that the story? Cleopatra had to kill herself because Octavius was the victor and Marc Antony the loser? So that was the end of the long reign of Pharoahs. And it ended in suicide. What a chilling ending. Only a woman could have been that brave. They were over. Cleopatra Over she should have been named.

She breathed deeply. The air was so wonderfully fresh and moist here. It helped. The channel was still and smooth and flowed with hardly any noticeable surface motion. It was smoky looking and gave itself over to this type of quiet and still meditation.

Suddenly, as she stared at the glassy still surface, the nostrils, ears and eyes of a hippo lifted just above the the water.

"William," she said, not as a question but as an expression of astonishment.

And then he was gone. She stood up in surprise. The appearance and disappearance had been so subtle and quiet it was hard to believe and she doubted for a moment that she had seen it. But the proof was in the little ripples left behind on the surface of the channel. Was that William? Had she just seen Prince William? He lives in that river, she thought, but he won't try to come up here, will he? Is he here to kill me?

Just then, Nicole came around the corner from her "private" room up front and made a little jump when she saw Rebecca standing.

"Oh," she said, "Good morning Rebecca. You startled me."

"Good morning," Rebecca said without using a name, feeling once again, embarrassed and flustered by the proximity of a movie star and the requirement to participate in her make believe. "I just saw William," she said a bit awkwardly.

"Who's William?"

"The hippo that lives in the river."

"There's a hippo in the river?"

"Yes," she said, but didn't know how to finish or add to the conversation, and the strange feeling of being an alien was grabbing at her mind again.

She wanted to jump in the river to get away from Nicole Kidman.

"Are you feeling any better this morning?" Donna asked.

"Ummm," Rebecca said, tongue tied over nothing. She looked around but managed finally to look back at Donna, who was smiling at her, expecting an answer. "Yes," she finally said, and then added, "thank you."

"Would you like some coffee?" Donna asked as she walked over to the coffee table. Rebecca followed her out of some sort of instinct.

"Yes please," she said, having trouble believing that Nicole Kidman was about to make her a cup of coffee. "What is your friend's name again?" she asked.

"Bill."

"Right, right. I'll try to remember that. I mean it's not that I can't remember names or your name... which is Donna you said..."

Finally Rebecca, not able to talk under these conditions, blurted out, "I feel so funny talking this way, because if you admitted you were Nicole Kidman, then I could ask you questions about your work and acting, but since you're Donna I can't ask you anything. Because what would be the point?"

Oh dear, she thought, *what in the hell is wrong with me. I should have jumped in the river.*

"How would you talk to anyone else at this camp? Do you doubt what they're telling you?"

"I'm sorry," she said, but she couldn't leave it at that, "but with a stranger I would believe whatever they tell me about themselves because I have no proof they're lying, but with you, because you're lying... well there isn't really anything to say."

"I'm not lying, Rebecca. My name is Donna. You're happy to call the hippo William. If you want I can call you Shelly and we can both pretend we're someone else."

"See? You said both."

"Excuse me," she said, rolling her eyes, and took two of the three coffees she had made and left back to go back to her room. "Enjoy your coffee," she said and added, "Please respect my privacy and don't speak to me again. Or I can ask Nann if you prefer."

Rebecca sat on the couch and moped. She rubbed her head and tried to make the weird "crooked" feeling go away. Her hands were shaking now, from the encounter.

I can't believe I just had a fight with Nicole Kidman.

"Good morning Miss Over," Marcel said, as he wandered in from the other direction. *Just what I need right now,* she thought. "Oh good morning Marcel," she sighed, trying to hold her hands steady.

"How did you sleep?" he asked.

"Fine thank you."

"Are you still ill?"

"No I think I'm fine now," she lied.

"But how can you be uncertain?"

"I'm... I'm not uncertain..."

"Think? Doesn't that mean you don't know?"

"Yes. I guess it's a little vague."

"In America, English is hardly spoken," he answered as he went over to the bar and behind it to get some cold water from the fridge.

I suppose that's today's America insult, she thought as she watched Marcel neglect to mark a tick on his drink bill, then go back down the path to his room without saying anything else.

She remained where she sat and did nothing but stare at the channel where the hippo had been. She tried to keep her mind from wandering or obsessing but it was hard. Within an hour everyone was up and ready for breakfast, but apart from answering, "I'm fine," Rebecca didn't talk to them much. She had to hold things together and not get into any fights with the movie star or Nann wouldn't take her to see the Carmine Bee Eaters.

Over breakfast Nann announced there would only be one excursion that day as it was quite a long one. She asked if that was alright with everyone and it was, so very soon after breakfast System was driving her boat, along with the Scottish couple and Donna and Bill (and how that must have annoyed Donna, Rebecca thought with an uncharacteristic gleefulness, to be placed in the same boat as Rebecca). Nann drove the other boat with the DeKoning family and Adam.

The trip up the river was long because the river was heavily coiled. Back and forth they drove with such huge turns it hardly felt like they were moving forward, but always doubling back on themselves. The birds were rustled from their Papyrus homes as they motored by; some white birds even flew along ahead of the boat – as if guiding it. Now and then Nann would give a shout or System would point at a large Crocodile on the bank of the river, which would always quickly slide into the water as they raced by. Rebecca wasn't feeling as paranoid as she had felt that morning; the movement of the boat and the air on her face seemed to help. But it still seemed to her as though the animals — especially the birds — were participating in her own drama, by leading them further up the river to whatever they were going to see. They were like bridesmaids, flower girls and ring bearers leading the procession. She had a very keen sense that she was being taken somewhere.

Her hair was catching in the wind and was probably a fright — but it made her think of Donna and she couldn't resist the urge to look back. My God, Rebecca thought after she turned around and got a surreptitious glance, she really is extraordinary. She was looking at the scenery and birds as their boat raced by — and her reddish blonde locks fluttered without coming apart too much — her blue eyes mirrored the sky — her cheeks were slightly flushed from the wind and... everything about her was like a gorgeous commercial.

Suddenly the boat slowed and came to a stop, which was just as well because Donna had asked for privacy and Rebecca didn't want to be caught staring at her. Nann pulled the other boat alongside theirs and said, "Right, We're just going to stop for a while and do some fishing. Who's up for catching a Tiger Fish?"

While others fished Rebecca decided that she would take the opportunity to apologize to Donna for the little fracas they had that morning. She went to the back and said as quickly and as unobtrusively as she could, "Excuse me. I just wanted to apologize for what I said this morning."

Donna looked at Rebecca, simply nodded her head, then turned her attention back to Bill's fishing. Rebecca, trying to hide a certain sheepishness, went back to her place near the front and waited. When offered a chance to fish she declined. Really there was nothing much more that she wanted to do other than to see the Bee Eaters. The feeling of being ill but not truly sick put her in a foul mood and made her feel like this safari needed to end as soon as possible. She had seen so much it could hardly be thought of as a failure just because the last two days were difficult.

Once they were on their way again, she felt a little better, again because of the movement and the rumble of the engine. They had to change gas tanks once, but eventually the two boats slowed as they drew closer to small cliffs on the right. Small red birds were fluttering all over the place and Rebecca's pulse quickened.

"System are those the Bee Eaters?" Rebecca asked.

System nodded and said, "Doze are de Carmine Bee Eatahs."

They drew alongside the cliff and stopped. The birds were a brilliant red, and they perched or clung to holes in the brown dry mud cliff which was about twenty feet high. They flew away after, she presumed, feeding the chicks hidden inside.

The holes reminded her of the little cubby holes in an old writing desk — pockets of secrets and ideas; possibilities; the hidden corners of a great mind. There were several large trees to either side of the cliff, growing at the water level, and these were also used as perches for the red birds.

She remembered her semi-wakeful dream she had on the plane, when all the birds stopped doing what they were doing and turned to stare at her. But these birds carried on, oblivious to their spectators. They worked tirelessly to feed their young and never once did a bird cast a curious glance in their direction.

They were so beautiful it almost seemed strange that they did nothing but tend to their nests or the babies inside their cubby holes. Their beauty felt completely irrelevant. In a way, this is what the star named Donna had to deal with every day. Being beautiful and looked at.

Marcel's camera was twicking away as usual, and he appeared to be directing Nann on where to position the boat. He had done this at every camp and every driver had obeyed him. It still puzzled her. She had remembered to bring her camera this time, almost willfully forgetting it until now, so she raised it and took her first picture of the trip. And then she decided that would be her only picture.

It was a bit anti-climactic, actually. She had said all those months ago (how it already felt like years) that she wanted to "bucket list" the Carmine Bee Eaters and now she had seen them. But like everyone, she overestimated the impact it would make on her feelings. To be sure, they were beautiful, but there was something strange and even a little unsettling about the way they ignored the tourists that were watching them.

After enough time spent ogling the birds, Nann announced that they were continuing upstream for a surprise. The boats started up again and drove for a few more minutes to the backside of a very steep hill. There was a small dock here — big enough for only one boat — so Nann parked her boat next to System's and they tied them together.

Rebecca hoped this surprise wasn't going to be a gimmicky kind of tourist thing, where supposedly "native" Africans do a traditional dance that they wouldn't do at their local watering hole, where instead they dance like everyone else in the world. The way she had been hustled through Maun by the American greeter was the first time she realized how much of a production it all was, and that she was not really seeing Africa but simply a packaged, tourist's version of Africa. They had been rushed through and pushed along at each step of the journey, and although it had truly been fantastic, (not to mention the sex with John), she didn't want the beauty of it all spoiled by local people performing like Jeffrey the Fish Eagle did yesterday.

"Now I presume," Nann said, "that you all know Botswana has the highest rate of AIDS in Africa? Well not the highest but close to it. Swaziland is highest. Here it's just about one out of three. But some of the youngsters, especially the boys, are abandoned by their families and they literally grow up on the streets. They've got no family at all. Some of the other boys are simply not wanted and abandoned for that reason. This place is called the Bana Ba Metsi School which means Children of the River in Setswana, and it's a place for boys at-risk. They take these boys and give them housing and an education and teach them a profession like brick laying or welding, up to the age of sixteen. So all the boys here are ten to fifteen years old, and as long as they behave they'll spend five years here learning how to take care of themselves. At sixteen they go back to society. It's all self supporting with donations, mostly from America. Anyway, Terrence has agreed to give us a tour of the facilities and then there'll be a special treat for us at the end."

This didn't sound like a tourist gimmick.

They walked up a very steep hill and then several hundred yards across a dry scrabbly piece of land until they came to a metal fence about fifteen feel high. The gate was open and they walked in and followed a long dirt supply road until they came to a cluster of buildings that looked like the main compound. It was a bit like the quad of a campus, except there were no trees nor grass — just pounded dirt.

Nann said she'd be right back and went to look for someone.

The place looked deserted and it gave Rebecca an eerie feeling as if they had just discovered a ghost town. There was a large unfinished building on one side — another smaller building painted green and blue, and a third which looked like a picnic shelter. She noticed then that there were people under the shelter and she relaxed a bit. That's where everyone was.

Nann returned with a white woman she introduced as Emma, and Emma explained to their group while Nann went off somewhere to do something, that it was "meeting time" — the time for everyone — both young and old, teacher and student — to sit down and talk through their problems. "And there are many," she added. In the meantime Emma was going to take them around to have a look at the school facilities.

As they walked in typical tourist formation from one building to another, like they would at a French chateau, Rebecca found herself clinging to the De Koning family rather than the pair of couples, who seemed to have formed one of those natural alliances that couples make. But this clinging was also in part, a reaction to the feeling this place was giving her. Unlike a chateau, it wasn't at all inspiring. Or at least she didn't feel it.

Everything looked sad and strange; filthy and dusty. The few adults she saw (and their tour guide Emma herself) looked haggard and worn out; twenty years older than they should look. The area for the butchery was too frightening for her to look very long on it, though her companions had no problem with the dried animal blood covering the butcher's table and the cutting and slicing and hacking instruments hanging on the walls. Marcel was happily clicking and twicking away. The chickens were kept in an enclosure that was to her mind, far too small and prison-like. The unfinished buildings Emma explained were part of the education process. The boys learned by doing, so they built the buildings they would live, learn and play in.

But the place felt oppressive. It was so much more difficult than anything she had to do back home. Once, she looked out into the grassy courtyard of her school and Mr. Dreyfus, the art teacher, was having his students paint the flowers of white clover with colors of their choice. That was what they did back home. They painted flowers and lived in a never never land where the big (presumably male) intelligent designer looked after things. But this was real. This was Darwinian and scary and alone. It was so horrible. She didn't feel inspired by anything at all, but just felt depressed that it existed. In one of the social rooms was a poster reminding them to take their HIV medication. Elsewhere were AIDS-related teaching and inspirational signs about respecting privacy, not discriminating, being nice, and so on.

But they were just boys here. Boys.

It was just too unfair. Too unfair. She felt tears start to well up but held them back. But that only made her jaw start to twitch, so she walked around with her hand over her mouth, probably looking like a horrified tourist which, in a way, was true, but not from disgust. It was from sorrow. And empathy. She pitied them.

Eventually the group, having made a large circle of the compound, were back where they had started. The "meeting time" had broken up and all the Botswanan boys were loping along toward the recreation room where she had seen the signs about what to do when you're told you have HIV. She had thought "when?" as they walked through the place. The posters say "when" you get HIV. Maybe they thought it was simply inevitable, like puberty.

Terence, the founder of the school, walked up with Nann and gave them a short talk about the boys and how he, an American, came to be living and running a place so far away from home. But all Rebecca wanted to ask was how he could stand it. The children looked like all unloved children.

Why me? That's the look they all had.

She wondered how the others felt; if they saw it as she did. She scanned their faces and of Anton and Griet, but her peers all looked very serious and very engaged in what Terence was saying about choice: the choice that each boy would have to make when it was time to leave here. They all, including the famous one, looked like concerned condescending Westerners while all she could feel about herself was that she was being rather atrocious at having this reaction.

Pull yourself together, she thought again. *Maybe I should just excuse myself and go back to the boat. I saw the Carmine Bee Eaters. I don't need to see this. But then Nann would be offended. She did this for us.*

She felt her right hand start to tremble again, and held it so that no one would notice.

Her group was suddenly moving then, and she realized she hadn't been paying attention — lost in her own thoughts. She couldn't remember a single thing Terence had said about the school or his history; how he started it. She felt like one of her inattentive misbehaving students. She moved along with the group as they walked toward the blue and green building which was the recreation room. Inside some of the boys had arranged themselves in front of a group of Xylophones. But that wasn't the right word. They were Marimbas, wooden or bamboo Marimbas — about seven of them altogether, plus one boy who had a drum on the ground.

"The other thing we do here," Terence said, "is this. This is our Marimba troop. Prince Harry's been here — I think he stayed at your camp if I'm not mistaken — but he actually flew these boys up to England to play at one of his birthday parties. Well not these boys but the boys who were here at the time. It's one of their favorite things. Fortune's the leader. Fortune, it's all yours mate."

Then, after the boy named Fortune made a nod of his head, suddenly, as loud as a night club, the boys started playing the Marimbas and the music it made exploded in the center of her heart and blasted all the horrible feelings away. She was instantly in awe and she looked over at Osiris and Iris who were sitting on the floor — smiles as big as hers and their eyes glittering like gemstones. Their parents were smiling too: everyone was smiling. Even Marcel looked happy and renewed.

She closed her eyes to let the music flow through her body and cleanse it of all its wickedness and the bad feelings she had been having. The music sounded like nothing she had ever heard — she had rarely heard live music anyway — but it sounded like all the feelings Africa had, until now, brought up in her. It sounded like the lion and the ostrich. It sounded like the hyena. It sounded like the cries of poor Beatrice who couldn't stand the killing, and like the lullabies she imagined her mother had sung to her in the short time they had together. She began to cry again — for all that she had missed and for all that she had. Then she opened her eyes again to watch the boys, who performed with an intensity that was unmatched by anything in her experience, ever in her life. The throaty, earthy, music gathered up the sunsets and the deaths and deposited both of them on the ground in front of her, in equal parts, and she could sense why people were inclined to pound the earth with their feet when they danced.

Afterwards, the tiny group of tourists applauded wildly, as did she. It felt like the greatest performance to have ever taken place in the history of the world. But what gave Rebecca the chills, was that while they applauded, the boys just stood behind their Marimbas and stared. None of them smiled.

Chapter 18

After the performance the tourists were led back to the large gated entrance of the school and they said goodbye to Terence and Emma, thanked them for a wonderful experience and asked where they could send donations. Rebecca was quiet and kept her thoughts and emotions in check, while the others were asking how they could donate money.

At the boats, once they were in their places, Nann said, "Right, we're just going to go back around the bend and there's a little bit of shore there. I don't know if you saw it on the way up but there's a Sausage tree there and it's a nice place to have a picnic. System please go on ahead of me would you? I've just got to change tanks."

So, this miserable isolated school apparently being as deep into Africa as they were going to go, the boats followed the slow current and went back down the river, around a few bends, until they were near the shore Nann talked about. System slowed the boat as he approached, but then he said, "Oh... what?" Then he stopped the boat completely.

Rebecca and the two couples turned to look at him. He was staring at the shore and he had a very puzzled, almost worried look. He reversed the boat's engine and they backed away from the shore. Rebecca looked at the shore, but all she could see were some large rocks and the big Sausage tree that Nann had mentioned.

"Is there a lion?" Rebecca asked.

"No," System said, "it is a boach."

Now what the hell is a boach, she thought, impatiently. System turned around and whistled and waved at Nann when her boat came around the bend with the DeKoning family and Adam. System's whistle hurt Rebecca's ears.

"What is it System!?" Nann shouted, and he pointed to the shore. Nann used her binoculars to look as she drew her boat alongside theirs. "Oh for fuck's sake," she said, "Awww no man. For fuck's sake. Dammit!"

"What is it?" Marcel asked.

"It's an Ellie," she answered.

Rebecca looked back at the shore but saw no elephant. But as the boats inched closer to the shore, what she had thought were some rocks turned out to be a carcass. The skin was dark grey and it had dried so that it was now draped across the bones like a strange limp cloth. She couldn't tell what part was what.

"I'll have to fly to Maun tomorrow to make a report. Aww shame man."

Bill asked why she had to report it.

"It's been poached," Nann said, "he didn't die, he was killed."

Poached, Rebecca thought, and shuddered. As Nann started to explain everything, images poured through her mind, of an elephant, lying on its side, still alive, while poachers in army fatigues hacked away at the parts they wanted. It made her very light headed and she started to go faint. She put her head down and the feeling passed, but she kept her head down for a few seconds more until she could look up at Nann, who was circling the giant carcas and pointing.

"You see there," she said, indicating a masticated area around what had been the head, "You can see how the tusks were cut out of the bone there. You see those hacking marks? And here is where the ears were — they take those too — and the eyes as well. They use the eyes for Muti. Do you know what Muti is? Witchdoctor stuff. They use human organs for medicine — usually children that they murder. There was a murder here in Bots about ten years ago. Everyone found out about it and they found the poor boy's organs but the police destroyed them before they could be DNA tested. Corruption eh? It's everywhere. Ya, but they use animal parts and trees parts too. It's all superstitious nonsense, but not everyone believes in western medicine."

Rebecca looked at the others while Nann was speaking, trying not to think about what she was saying. She tried to shut her ears. Poachers and witch doctors and children's organs. When she glanced over at the movie star, that actress snapped her head quite suddenly as if she felt Rebecca's offensive gaze. And then this famous woman said, "Murderer."

"Murderer," she said to Rebecca, and then she turned back to pay attention to Nann as she explained the various things that had happened to the elephant.

"What?" Rebecca asked, but Nicole did not respond or turn around. Was she calling her a murderer?

"I didn't do it," she said, defensively, and they, the other four passengers in the boat, turned and looked at her with quizzical looks. Rebecca looked away from them, aware that she might be causing a scene. She had just wanted to defend herself, but of course that made no sense at all. How could she murder an elephant? And why would Nicole say that she had? Did she mishear her?

"Well," Nann said, not noticing anything that had just happened, "we'll just have to picnic on the boats. We'll drift down the river for a bit. If you want to fish you can fish. Does anyone want to swim?"

"Swim? Are you joking? There are crocodiles in the river Nann!" Rebecca shouted.

The thought of swimming made her panicky again.

"It's alright Rebecca, they're not everywhere and we always do a careful inspection before going for a dip."

"But what about the hippos?"

Nann sighed, but did so patiently. "We're not going to have you swimming with hippos either."

"No," Rebecca stated flatly, as if being asked to do something, "No, no, no, no. Absolutely not."

"You don't have to swim if you don't want to."

"But I don't want anyone..." She took a breath and held it because she was aware that everyone was staring at her with those same quizzical looks. She had wanted to say that she didn't want anyone else to swim either, because she didn't want to see anyone get eaten.

"But what about the sharks?" she finally asked when she couldn't finish her original question. Everyone laughed at her. Nicole was laughing at her too. She was looking at the floor of the boat and snickering to herself with her fingers lightly touching her beautiful lips.

Bitch.

"I think it's safe to say," Nann said, "that there are no sharks in Botswana. We're land locked."

"But there are fish in Botswana!" she shouted, annoyed that they thought she was stupid. But she caught herself and followed it up with, "I'm sorry."

"There are no sharks in the river," Nann said quietly and firmly, and it was hard to miss the meaning of her tone.

Pull yourself together, Rebecca said to herself for the third time that day, and tried once again, to reign in her emotions. She suddenly realized she was acting like Beatrice from the other camp when she was crying about the baby deer. She must have been sick from Lariam too. But nobody realized she was suffering.

They drifted down the river and ate lunch, drank tea or coffee or juice or water. Rebecca felt herself calm down again, probably because of their slow lazy movement down the river and the bright warm sun on her face. At one point, the actress screamed "ahh" when a butterfly fluttered near her face. *Flutterby*, Rebecca thought, *She's scared of a silly flutterby.*

The two men in her boat fished for a while and when a swimming place was found and inspected all four of them went swimming. Nicole/Donna had been wearing a plain white shirt over a blue kikhoi — a traditional Botswanan fabric which could be used for bundling food or as a makeshift skirt or a head scarf. She removed both pieces to reveal her slender lithe body under a shiny light blue one-piece bathing suit — a very frosty color that was out of place here where everything was taupe or green and muted, except for the birds.

Oh, Rebecca thought, *the birds*. That's what she looks like — like a strange beautiful bird. What was that story John told us around the fire about Beauty? *Beauty lived on a branch of a tree. And the lion and the hyena both wanted her, but they couldn't reach her. And so jealous they were they tried to kill each other in order to have her all to himself. But they ended up mortally wounding each other and they both died. And Beauty had never once looked down at them and didn't know any of this had happened.*

She day-dreamed about this story while the others swam and then she thought about the even more pleasant time she had later when John showed up at her porch with that round expectant boyish face of his. Please let me in, it said, she remembered, and then the way he stood there with his dark hairy chest and his erection pointing at her like... what was that phrase... always pointing up at you like a hat rack. She giggled — she thought it was an Irish expression but wasn't sure — and then she remembered the great satisfaction she gained when he slipped it in and they were... complete... for the most part — at least as far as everything that had gone on that night — all the fireside chatter and looks and what not — banished doubts about his wife Sarah — all felt that it was finally satisfied when the two of them were together.

And how different to the feeling of her father, which had always felt like a piece of wood scraping against chapped flesh.

That was one of the reasons she had liked sex in that period when guys were still abundant. There was a kind of subconscious sense, perhaps, that she could banish the terrible physical feeling with the good one. And in a way, it had. It had been quite healing, being promiscuous; she couldn't deny it, and didn't want to except for judgmental people like Julian's friend Bruce The Low who had once said that a woman who aborts was unnatural. Oh she wanted to kill him that night. Was that last Thanksgiving?

While having these thoughts, she had been staring vacantly at the two couples swimming about in a shallow part of the river, the two boats making a kind of cove around them, when, from her angle and because of the angle of the sun off the water she thought she saw a crocodile moving toward the swimmers.

There was, in fact, a crocodile moving toward them.

She stood up, knocking over her can of lemonade and shouted, "Nicole watch out!"

Everyone looked at her when she shouted and then looked to where she was pointing. But it was just a large piece of papyrus floating on the surface of the river.

"Sorry," she said, "Oh my God. I thought it was a crocodile. I was so scared."

When the Papyrus floated by the other boat, Nann reached down and plucked it out of the water. "Just Papyrus," she said, "We have a lot of that here, Rebecca, as you can see." She sounded annoyed and Rebecca vowed not to speak to her or anyone else for the rest of the trip, except to say goodbye tomorrow. Her safari was nearly over and it had been a hard trip in spite of the luxury, and she wasn't sure what it was all about or why she had even taken it. Because her principal didn't believe in evolution? That didn't make sense. Because she was tired of her relationship with Julian? How could she be tired of him when she loved him?

Her heart was still racing from what she thought was a close encounter with a crocodile, when suddenly she felt herself blanch inside while all the blood drained from her face. The epiphany she had was as unexpected as one of those rare bolts of lightning that come out of a clear cloudless sky, like the sky today. Except it had always been there.

She sank a little bit; her heart dropped from a sickening kind of feeling when she understood what had been bothering her for so long. She looked over at the children; the little gods sired by the silly Marcel DeKoning. They smiled back at her, as they had been doing all week, and she knew too why they had been smiling all week. They weren't judges. They weren't gods. They were the cherubs that were there to help her when it came time to be judged. When she was taken before her executioner, whoever he turned out to be, they were there to hold her hands and escort her to the prisoner's box to comfort her while she was sentenced.

Because she had killed her father.

She had fed him the drugs that ended his life early. And she had done it without his permission, without telling him, and that is murder.

The doctor had told her, not the patient, on the last day of his treatment, that the cancer was everywhere: his liver, lungs, colon, and that it was a matter of a month or two, at the very most. And everyone thought he was getting better. Aunt Vicky. Willard Over himself. Julian. Principal Blount. Even she herself had thought he was getting better until the doctor gave her the news. Everyone thought he was part of the four percenters — that horribly small percentage of people who survive the deadliest of all cancers.

But he wasn't. He wasn't that special. He wasn't anything special. Just uninformed — not wanting to know the truth; using her to stare at it instead like someone closing his eyes at a movie and asking what happened. That was how he drew her back into his lair; making her face the bitter truths while he just sat there making sculptures with his damned baked potato and pats of butter and ignorantly insisting every single day that he was "beating it."

And when she had asked him "why did you do that to me" and he had bowed his head in shame and mumbled 'I don't know,' she had decided that night to end his life. She told herself it was the right thing to do, since he was just going to wind up dying a brutal horrible death in a palliative care facility on the edge of town designed for suffering and dying, hopefully with haste. But it was disgust that moved her, not compassion. It was disgust and anger and rage, all quietly contained for decades, like a genie in a lamp, until rubbed. She had lied to herself and told herself she was being strong hearted and merciful and she had made herself believe it all this time. The doctor had given her the prescriptions which she said Rebecca could use when the right time came. But the time came a few months early. And now God was ready to make her pay. And she, she now knew, was ready to pay too.

Chapter 19

It occurred to her, while she was resting beneath her mosquito netting before dinner, lying on her back, trying to make the spinning, trapped, and guilt-ridden feeling in her head go away, that when she had shouted at the swimmers, warning them that they were about to be drowned and dismembered by a reed of Papyrus, she had shouted "Nicole" instead of "Donna" and nobody questioned her about it, including Nicole herself. Nobody said, "Who the hell is Nicole?"

So they were all a bunch of liars, she thought, even Nann.

"Further proof is not required," she said aloud, and rolled over onto her stomach and tried not to think about the fact that they were all in on it together, perhaps even the DeKoning family. Everyone had been told but she, that it was, in fact, Nicole Kidman who had looked at her with that intense stare she is capable of making and called her a murderer.

"Nicole Kidman has accused me of murder," she said as she rolled over onto her back again. "Or at least someone who looks like her. Oh but Julian she's right. If only I could tell you. You're the one I wanted to tell, not John. John was... John was..."

She remembered once again his handsome face hovering in the dark, staring up at her from down below. Like Beauty in the tree. She was Beauty on the porch. And sometimes we beautiful creatures look down at the poor men and say yes, come up, come up. But we never know why. Had she inadvertently signaled her father, somehow, to enter her room?

She was awfully dense about certain things that everyone else seemed to know by instinct.

Maybe she had given a signal she wasn't aware of.

She had always blamed the lack of... mother.

I don't know. That's all he could say.

She had, indeed, after the oncologist had told her the truth about his condition, considered the terrible suffering he was going to experience as the cancer devoured his organs. She considered first the good relationship they had before all the dark matter, when she was a pre-pubescent girl. He would take her to Cascade Park and encouraged her to play with the other children. He played baseball with her and taught her how to bunt which, he said, was one of the secrets of playing good baseball. He taught her how to throw a football, and how to play "tag" football so she wouldn't get hurt. And he helped her with girl things, too, like dolls and cooking soup or spaghetti sauce. It pained her to think of that man suffering the pain of end stage cancer.

But then she considered the dark side. The erotic side. Was it erotic? Whatever caused him to do that, one thing was certain: that his feelings about her had changed and whatever he assumed was not what she assumed. And that man, the rapist, she could only think that the suffering he was bound to have was his just reward. But the work of letting him suffer as he died would, of course, fall mostly upon her.

They would remove his colon, perhaps, and then she'd have to be there helping empty his colostomy bag because he wouldn't want to do it himself. Or he'd suffocate as less and less lung was available for oxygen. She'd have to help him out of his chair and to walk across the room to the fridge, just as she had been helping him take short walks to his garden and back. Then they'd have to set up a bed downstairs or move him to the dying facility. He wouldn't even have the strength to sit up but would just lie there with his mouth open, pissing and shitting in his diapers, making her clean it up, or she would have to hold his penis so he could pee in the bed pan thing. And then finally he would look like a cadaver before he became one, begging her with his eyes to end his suffering — his eyes telling her, "I just can't do it myself."

There had been terrible moments, in the weeks after the oncologist told her the truth, when she just wanted to drive him to the cemetery and leave him there.

Finally, she decided it was the right thing to do.

But she wasn't sure anymore why she did it then, at that moment. That evening.

She couldn't say if she was good or bad, merciful or mean.

What's in a month? What's a month of life?

But it was his month. His life.

No it wasn't. Not really. It was a month of my life too.

Why did you do that? I asked.

I don't know, he said.

Why did you do that?

I don't know.

WELL KNOW!

She imagined screaming this where he sat at the kitchen table, in front of his baked potato, the butter slowly melting into yellow slits.

I don't know, was still his answer. He went to the grave, and it was always the only answer.

*

Her last dinner in Africa was the usual fabulous meal. She was so used to these nice meals it didn't even surprise her anymore. She felt ravenous after the long day and also because one of the strange feelings she was now having was constant hunger. The chat around the table was subdued, but she thought she heard Marshall or Eloise or whatever their names were — she was getting even more confused — say something about it being their last supper.

"Here's something I've never understood," she said to the table, "Why is it called 'The Last Supper'? Why isn't it called 'The Last Dinner'? Or the 'The Last Meal' which is what most prisoners facing execution get? That supper word, I've just never understood it. He is the King, right? Kings don't have suppers they have dinners. And in the original Italian the proper translation is 'dinner.' So how did it become 'supper' anyway?"

No one answered, until the actress, who was sitting at the other end of the table said, "Interesting."

"What's interesting?" Rebecca asked strongly, almost snappishly.

"What you just said," the actress said.

"How can you can say it's interesting when you're not even who you say you are?"

The actress put her fork down forcefully on the plate, but kept the knife gripped firmly in her hand. This small gesture wasn't lost on Rebecca.

"Nann," the actress said, smiling but angry, "I really don't think I can stand much more of this."

"Rebecca..." Nann said, trying to intercede, "Please darling? Please try to calm down."

Rebecca saw that she was misbehaving, again, and when she looked at Nann she saw in her face the look she would give her students when they were just one more word away from being sent to the principal's office.

Feeling stupid, she looked over at Donna (and she decided instantly that she would never again question her), and said, "I'm so sorry Donna. I don't know what's... I've been having a lot of strange feelings today. I think I probably just wished you were famous so I could ask for an autograph for my friend Julian who adores you. I mean her. The actor."

"It's probably the Lariam sickness," Nann said.

"Yes," Rebecca agreed, but not really sure, "probably that's what it is."

She looked at Donna and Bill, the Scottish couple, then the two children, Elizabeth and then finally Marcel, who, to no great surprise, had not stopped eating during her short outburst and stared back at her while he munched on asparagus spears. She looked across at System and Adam, and then finally at Nann. "I think I'd better go to bed," she said.

She rose from the table and walked slowly over to the path which led to their bungalows. It was considerably darker than the lounge and the firepit nearby, and she was suddenly frightened again. She could only see a few feet of the path before her. She began to tremble because everything seemed to go even darker around the edges as she looked at it.

"I don't want to go in there," she shouted to no one in particular.

Nann shouted, "Just turn on your torch Rebecca."

She was shaking violently, but did as she was told. She felt like all thumbs trying to push the button to turn on the flashlight, but managed. She held the light with two hands, shoved the puny beam ahead of her and advanced a yard, but the light seemed to illuminate nothing. It seemed weak against the much more powerful darkness she was walking into, and she shouted, "I can't! I can't!" She was shaking so much she dropped the flashlight, and then she thought she saw something move and yelled, "Help me!" She was about to sink onto her knees but then she felt a hand on her back and she jumped.

It was Marcel. "What is your problem?" he asked. He bent down and picked up her flashlight, then looked at her, waiting for an answer. "Well?" he demanded again.

"I don't know," she said. As Marcel helped her walk down the path by holding her elbow, she thought about how she had just given him her father's answer. "I don't know."

Marcel, showing the first bit of civility since she met him a week ago, escorted her all the way to her bungalow, except that he sounded distracted and irritated in having to do it. "Would you please watch where you place your feet," he said, but in a punitive tone, and when they were standing in front of the curtain of her room, he sighed wearily and said, "Are you competent again?"

"Yes Marcel, thank you," she said. And then she thought of a question she wanted to ask. She should have asked him before and might have avoided all of this. "Marcel, before you go, can I ask you a question?"

"I don't know, *can* you?"

"Do you think she is Nicole Kidman?" she asked.

"I do not care," he said. "I will take your torch to light my way back." And then he left. She thought his answer was genius, and it completely calmed her down.

Inside her room she undressed to be completely naked and sat on her bed under the mosquito netting with the side table lamp on. The lamp was solar powered and quite weak — not strong enough to use for reading — but she didn't feel like being in the dark just yet. She was silent, not the least bit tired, and for once, her mind wasn't filled with racing thoughts. There was something about the "I don't know" answer she gave to Marcel that knocked all the fight out of her.

Why had she chosen that day, anyway?

After his last chemo treatment (which they had all thought had been successful), Dr. Yoshida had asked Rebecca to come into her office to talk, while her father waited with the other cancer patients. Dr. Yoshida had stunned her with the news that her father was done with his treatment and was not going to live, and then she stunned Rebecca a second time when she said there were options for her and her father to consider.

"You don't have to do this," Dr. Yoshida had said, when explaining the "elixir" process of assisted suicide, "but it is an option I offer — as a person, not a doctor. I can write you a prescription for the drugs. Or you can just let nature take it's course, and he can self administer morphine for any pain."

Rebecca interrupted, "He won't self administer anything,"

"Well then you should expect it to be painful and that he will suffer horribly. Most people don't want their loved ones to suffer, but I understand it's also one of the hardest things in the world for someone to do in order to alleviate their suffering. You'll have to talk about it with your father."

She was supposed to give him one drug to settle his stomach before giving him the pentobarbital to drink, mixed with some sort of fruit juice that he liked.

She did it just after his 'last supper' of tomato soup and toast. She put the first drug in his soup.

Then they acted out his evening ritual for one final time. She had helped the supposedly healthy man to his bedroom and she had helped him dress into his pajamas.

"You don't have to do this anymore daughter, I'm feeling stronger all the time."

"I want to do it," she had said.

And then she had left the room and returned with some cranberry juice. Before she lifted his legs into his bed and tucked him in, she had said, "Father, the doctor said you need to drink this," and handed him the glass.

"What is it?" he had asked.

"It's pentobarbital mixed with cranberry juice," she had said, telling an absolute truth she knew he wouldn't understand. "It's to put you to sleep, and the cranberry juice helps disguise the taste."

And he had drunk it, not questioning anything. She lifted his legs under the covers and tucked him in. He said, "Goodnight daughter."

And Rebecca had said, "Goodnight father."

He closed his eyes and was asleep almost immediately.

She took from his side table a stethoscope she had purchased and hidden there. She sat on the side of his bed, opened his pajama shirt and began listening to his heartbeat.

It beat about twenty times, gradually slowing.

And then it stopped.

She buttoned his shirt; pulled the blanket up under his arms.

She turned off the light on his bedside table, and then she turned off the overhead lights and shut his door.

She took a seat at his kitchen table.

She didn't move an inch until dawn, and she thought of absolutely nothing.

In the morning she stood, stiff and aching, and walked into his bedroom to "discover" that he had died during the night. It was then that she was suddenly struck by the loss and she sank to the floor in sobs, crying, "Father, Oh father, Oh my dear father."

And then everything started up again. The cremation. Aunt Vicky. Her feelings about Julian. School. The trip to Africa.

But now, here at Nxamasere, it all seemed so ambiguous. She wasn't sure if she had been kind or vengeful. It would have been more cruel to let him suffer. And she certainly couldn't have involved Aunt Vicky or that part of the family in the decision because they were the type to think of death as a failure — something you had to fight against every minute of every day, and attribute to the devil — the Death Be Not Proud gang — and if she had told her father the truth, would he have gone along with it? Unlikely. He seemed much more happy having her come over every night; drawing her back into that house.

She then heard the crack of a couple of branches outside her room. The curtain was drawn, but her heart was suddenly beating fast again. She lifted the mosquito net and stepped out of the bed. She heard some more crackling branches and for a moment she thought it might be a person. "Nann," she said through the curtain, "Marcel?"

But the only answer was more crunching branches. It wasn't a loud noise or rapid. It just sounded like there something was moving slowly on the other side of her curtain. She made a crack between the two halves like she had the night before and she carefully peered through it.

And there he was.

Just ten feet from her room stood William, the young male hippo that had been driven from his birthplace by his father.

He was enormous. He was extraordinarily fat. It was hard to believe that something so large could actually walk. He was surprisingly pale in the moonlight that shone on his skin. Rebecca gasped when she first realized what she was looking at, but it wasn't so much from fear as from something else ---- something like recognition. He was another creature and utterly, vastly, different. But the same too. A creature. A creature. He was a creature. And so was she.

Without thinking about what she was doing, impulsively, she slowly pushed the two curtains all the way to the sides, and she quietly, stepped out of her room, completely naked, just as William was, and pale in the moonlight, like he was. Her breasts hung low, like the elephant's that she had seen, and her tummy protruded a bit, like the monkey's. She didn't have the false testes like the hyenas, but with every part of her body exposed, she felt as naked as the beasts she had seen and the beast in front of her.

She took two small steps toward William and stopped. "Father," she said, "if you want to kill me... do it now. Please."

The hippo stared at her, or appeared to stare at her. She had noticed on this trip that the eyes of most of the animals were extremely indifferent to humans. It was as if they didn't actually notice the humans or couldn't see them. But with William, it felt like he was staring at her, probing her, questioning her, and making an assessment. She felt he was as smart as she was. His tiny ears twitched like antennas and his glinting eyes scanned her. Then finally, in an extremely threatening gesture which made her start to cry out but soundlessly, he opened his mouth wide — impossibly wide — as wide as anything she had ever seen. His upper and lower jaws were like two halves of a giant clam, and he showed Rebecca the terrifying inside of his throat and his gigantic mouth and his teeth and the incisors that were almost a foot long and would go right through her body if that's what he chose. He shook his head with his mouth open in a semi-circular, back and forth motion and then he made a horrible grunting sound that was absolutely terrifying.

She held her breath because she was sure he was going to charge and kill her. She wanted to close her eyes but didn't. And she was ready. She was terrified, and she started to turn her head and started to cry because she was sure the attack was coming.

But he didn't attack. Instead, after the threatening demonstration was over, as if he had shown her, the human being, what he, the animal, was *capable* of doing, the beast William turned around and walked down the little bank, back into the water of the channel, where he disappeared, almost without a ripple.

After she could breath again, Rebecca returned to her bungalow and dressed in the clothes she was wearing at dinner. She wasn't sure what she had just done or why she had done it, but she felt that she didn't want to be alone. She needed some company. She was trembling and it took a few minutes to calm down. This was probably the most frightening thing she had ever done in her life. And foolish too. She packed her suitcase and prepared for her departure the following morning by making sure her passport and ticket were easily accessible. She was looking forward to going home and it occurred to her, looking at her passport with its two stamps, that thousands, if not tens or hundreds of thousands of people, went in and out of America every single day, and that the passport was rubbish.

"We don't really go anywhere," she said looking at her passport, "it all comes with you."

She walked back to the lounge. The dark path which had frightened her before no longer had any effect on her. The other guests were gathered around the fire pit, including Donna and Bill, and they were listening to Marcel talk about his career. She said, when she interrupted them, as an explanation, that she couldn't sleep and didn't want to waste her last night in Botswana by sleeping.

There was a bit of awkwardness, because of what had happened earlier at the dinner table, but she stayed quiet and eventually the fireside chatter started again and she was accepted into the tiny community. She didn't tell the others that she would never be able to take another trip like this again; that she had spent all the extra money she had; or that she was a poorly paid school teacher and the signs didn't look good for public servants in the near future. This was probably the only great trip she would ever be able to take. She stared at the others warmly – even at Donna, but she didn't interject to explain some important detail about a picayune fact. She didn't tell them of her close encounter with William. She told no one about her long struggle to reconcile herself to her father and what he had done to her and what she had done to him. She said nothing about herself because she felt, for that one terrifying, amplified and breathless moment standing naked in front of William the Hippo, that she had been completely herself, like all the animals she had seen that week. She had faced a killer, having been a killer herself. And she was then, in that moment, like all the animals she had seen, who suffer no doubts or qualms or pangs of guilt — perfect.

She sat by the fire and got along with the others of her species. She listened to them tell their stories and lies. She grinned and nodded when Donna talked about her home in Sydney. She was enormously surprised (but kept it to herself) when Marcel revealed that he was a world class photographer and famous in his own country. She accepted Elizabeth's offer of a photographic portrait which Marcel would take tomorrow before they all left the camp — standing in a traditional Botswanan mekorro — something akin to a thin canoe — in front of the Papayrus he said; Elizabeth said she would mail it to her after taking her address. Even more surprising and happy, Nann handed her a note with an address in Cape Town for John and Sarah Potgieter. Nann said had been called in over the radio earlier from Mombo. They had forgotten to pass it along.

And then she listened with great deep satisfaction and a sense that she had heard all of this before and was now a pro, as Nann talked about the many dangerous things that had happened "here in Bots," not knowing that something dangerous had just taken place a few yards from here a few minutes ago. She didn't feel smug about it. She simply felt that her mind was finally clean again.

And tomorrow, she knew, she would say goodbye to the DeKoning family and to Nann, Donna, the Okavango Delta and Maun. Tomorrow she would stare out of her Maun-to-Johannesburg jet window, down at the river, as it continued to flow into the immense Kalahari desert. Tomorrow she would stare in wonder as that river, which brought so much raw and new life to this region, disappeared in a line of puddles that stretched for half a mile or so until any evidence of the river vanished below the sand. Tomorrow, she knew, she would board the plane in Johannesburg and travel sixteen hours in a prison-like blood-clot inducing seat. And she knew she would have trouble sleeping and she would inspect her neighbor's scalp out of boredom. Tomorrow she would go back to Illyria, in Ohio, in America, and cope with the Christian fundamentalist principal who didn't want her to teach evolution, and an annoying Aunt who was not likely to stop being annoying anytime soon, and a best friend who was gay and sometimes insensitive to her feelings. Tomorrow she would do all of this, because tonight, they were all sitting around a fire, telling stories.

Chapter 20

Illyria

Julian LeFrere was trying to do his laundry before driving to the airport to pick up Rebecca, but he found himself constantly putting it off because he had been up all night having sex and was working on just a couple hours of sleep. But even as he replayed the night in his mind, remembering the shape of the guy's beautiful butt and how he had raised it in the air in a kind of begging action that turned Julian on much more than actually satisfying him; even as Julian laughed to himself that he could remember the guy's ass but not his name; even as he thought about how marvelous, erotic, thrilling and so on last night had been, there was something in his consciousness that was behaving like a mental blister. And it was getting worse. It had started Friday morning, bugged him a little on Saturday, disappeared while he was drinking and dancing and picking up this kid, but, oddly, returned on a few occasions during the sex, and was now nagging at him almost relentlessly.

Friday morning he had picked up his mail as usual, before heading to his classroom to enjoy half an hour of peace and quiet with his coffee and the Illyria Chronicle Telegram. He cherished this early morning solitude and savored every minute of it before turning his attention to his wonderful students for the rest of the day. And it was, indeed, the rest of the day. That was not an exaggeration. He and Rebecca often

commiserated on how much work they actually had to do —
sometimes even after supper he'd have to return to grading
exams or writing lessons, or he'd have to read up again on what
he was supposed to know in order to be able to tell his children
what they were supposed to know, like the capitals of the states
or the names of all the presidents: two things he couldn't
remember himself.

But he loved his students and all their noise and acting —
and he wouldn't give this job up for the world. He loved their
different temperaments and their colors. He especially loved
the shy ones — always wondered what it was that made them
shy. It was like they didn't want to let anyone in, and he always
wanted to try to break through the reservation. Sometimes,
though, he was absolutely astonished, like when he saw Philip
Myers — the little boy he and Rebecca jokingly referred to as
Little Miss Myers — walk into his classroom on the first day
carrying a purse.

In this highly conservative town it was almost unbelievable
to see a little self assured gay fifth grade boy walking around
with a purse, but it was even more incredible to see that Philip
was never teased or bullied about it. Julian knew that he-
himself was queer from as early an age as he could remember.
He remembered scoping out the boys when he was in the third
grade — not for sex at that age but for something undefined,
like hugging or rolling around on the ground and lying on top
of each other. At that age, his desire for other boys was barely
defined, but he still knew to keep it to himself.

But what had changed between the generations? He didn't know. Somehow, outside of his own understanding of what one had 'to do' to get by, Little Miss Myers carried a purse in addition to his backpack, and none of the other children said a single word about it.

As a gay male teacher Julian knew he had to keep his personal life to himself — very much to himself — which was why he did everything in Cleveland and only went to other guy's homes for sex. Of course there was no gay culture or even secret gay bars in Illyria so he had no choice in the matter, but if there was a choice he would have gone to Cleveland anyway. This job was far more important to him than being "out," even though it made him feel a little backwards and closeted, a little left out of his community. There were times when he wondered why he couldn't teach as an openly gay man; why they couldn't all just get along.

But then this is where Rebecca had been such a relief as a friend. Other teachers 'knew and did not know'. Rebecca 'knew and knew'. She knew immediately after they had met at the bar and she had asked him bluntly, and without any judgment whatsoever, if he preferred men. She was the most blunt person he had ever met, but never unkind or, at least, he didn't think she was being unkind.

Actually, it was sometimes hard to tell. At Thanksgiving a couple of months ago, at the dinner table, she had asked Bruce the Low if he was "still studying for his high school equivalency diploma," but she had asked it with such a straight and innocent face, not revealing any bit of anger or sarcasm, that nobody at the table was sure if she was cracking a joke, being mean or being serious. Least of all Bruce, who immediately lied that he graduated in the top ten percent of his class. Someone else at the table said, "Oh sure, top ten percent in cock sucking," and Bruce The Low had said, "Thank you darling." The raucous, slightly drunken, laughter around the table made everyone forget the odd sincerity of Rebecca's question, and he had forgotten to ask her later if she was joking or serious or being mean.

But it was that — her dispassionate honesty — that had been such a relief. It was as if he had walked into a room full of "true" when he met her, so that he was able to talk about anything, like Little Miss Myers.

"I'll never understand it," he had said, "why the other boys don't tease him for carrying that purse."

"Maybe you've never seen them tease him."

"True. But they all seem to like him."

"Well whatever it is," Rebecca had said, "you know it's got to be to their advantage *not* to tease him. Men and boys attack everything that's not of use to them."

But he had never figured it out — could never figure out — what use Philip was to the others. And at this point he no longer cared and was actually starting to dislike the boy. He'd see one of the bullies, like Bart Smith, demand some gum and Philip would open his little red purse and give him a stick. And then Julian would walk to the back, say, "You know there's no gum in my classroom," hold out his hand and demand that Bart spit it out which Bart would do with as much saliva as possible. And Julian would turn and look down at Philip because he would feel a distinct smirk coming from him. It made Julian feel that he wasn't getting it. It made him think that Philip understood more about his generation than he did – as if being a child in his day, had nothing to do with being a child now.

Friday morning had been no different from any other morning. He had picked up his mail from the front office, opened his classroom door, dropped his coat over the back of his yellow pine chair, sat down and had a gulp of coffee, then rifled quickly through the mail and memos to see if there was anything important before reading the paper, which would only take a few minutes anyway, since it was so sparse and mostly filled with farm news and high school sports. Then he noticed an envelope without a return address. He frowned when he saw it, opened it and removed a piece of neatly folded stationery. There was nothing particularly strange about it, until he unfolded it, and saw that it was written on his school's letterhead, and centered in the exact middle of the page, someone had typewritten, "People Are Complaining." That was all. Initial caps, but he didn't know if that meant anything. He stared at the letter aghast.

People Are Complaining

What people? What were they complaining about? But then, being addressed to him, it was specific enough that he could take it as a warning that someone was going to or had already filed a complaint. And of course, his sexuality seemed like the most likely thing they would attack, if they knew about it.

Then he told himself that "people" probably weren't complaining at all because if they were, someone would have said so. "People" didn't complain about him, they liked him. He had lived, in fact, his entire life knowing that he was very well liked. Even in the hardest year of school (the year Rebecca taught) he would see a group of students picking on some lonely kid and feel a weird relief that he was very well liked and that sort of thing couldn't happen to him.

So it couldn't be important, this note, and he shouldn't give it any thought. And that's what he told himself before tossing the note in his briefcase and getting ready for his kids. "I am very well liked," he said, "nobody is complaining."

But the shell had cracked.

He graded papers that night and only thought about the letter once or twice, and then twice more on Saturday, before hitting Cleveland with his friends, drinking, laughing, dancing and then picking up that guy, going to his place, leaving at dawn. But today he couldn't keep it out of his head and before doing his laundry, he retrieved the letter and looked at it again, as if the words would look different after looking at them a second time, and say, "People Love You," instead of "People Are Complaining."

But it wasn't different, of course, and he felt more troubled by it this time, as if his initial reaction of bravado was just a form of denial. Obviously, not everyone likes me, he thought, and he felt a terrible deflated feeling come over him that he had never felt before.

He decided then, that the only proper thing to do was to show the letter to the principal, as a precaution, even though it was on his school's letterhead and she herself might have been the one to send it, if she had some sort of hostility that he didn't know about. Mrs. Tyler hadn't expressed any dislike of him so he didn't think it was likely to be her. But he didn't think any of the other teachers had some sort of problem with him or his sexuality, assuming that's what the letter was about. Maybe it was one of the clerical people — one of the secretaries or the girl that was mostly in charge of making copies and counting the number of Ticonderogas in the closet.

But he didn't know why he thought it would be a clerk or a stock girl. It could have been a teacher. It might have been that horrible Mrs. Jackson with her awful blunt shoes and hideous burr-covered sweaters, who taught first graders, and had never said hello to him and, in fact, now that he thought about it, had a very suspicious way of making sure she didn't have to acknowledge him. She would leave the room if he came into it, or adjust herself to seem fully absorbed in some reading material. It was probably her, he thought. Yes, it was her. Mrs. Jackson sent the letter.

But his paranoia wasn't satisfied and he was about to start thinking on it again, while doing the preliminary sorting of his laundry on his living room couch, when he noticed there was a message on his answering machine. The answering machine was practically a dinosaur at this point because no one called his land line anymore, and he wanted to get rid of it and have everyone use his cell. But there was one person who had explained to everyone at his Thanksgiving dinner last year, that she didn't like to talk to people who were in motion, so she preferred not to use the cell.

Bruce The Low had answered her that night and said, "Well I'm not as angry as you Rebecca, I'm fine using cell phones. It's just another happy way of communicating." Rebecca explained that she wasn't the least bit angry about cell phones, she just liked to know that someone was listening. Bruce The Low had repeated, (because he wasn't listening), that he wasn't "as angry" as her. This annoyed Julian because although he thought it was a bit quirky, he understood her point of view and she was entitled to have it.

"And really," Rebecca had said, "everyone acts like they have to do this, that they have to buy a cell phone and talk while they're driving or talk while they're walking, but who says so? Who is making them do it? That's the real question. Technology is a form of bondage; enslavement by tchotchke consumerism."

Bruce pretended not to understand. Sometimes Julian felt really rather tired of Bruce even though he was the funniest friend he had. Bruce sometimes went to the mall, sat on a bench and shouted things at the confused elderly mall walkers, getting their exercise: "Looking good Betty!" "You're getting fatter Mr. Scott!"

When he saw the answering machine message indicator flashing "1" he knew who had left a message, and who was back from a trip to Africa that she said she had always wanted to take.

He pressed play and she shouted into the telephone as if there was a lot of noise around her.

"Hello Julian! I'm back and I'm in New York City at a pay phone. It's so noisy! I knew you wouldn't be home this morning so that's why I'm calling, because I'm in no danger of disturbing you. Did you have a nice time last night? I hope he was good looking, I want to hear all about it. Oh my God Julian, I had such an incredible time in Africa and I can't wait to tell you about it. I missed you so much, you have no idea, I really did. I often wished you had come with me, but then if you were with me I might not have gotten lucky myself, so maybe it worked out for the best."

She got laid?

"Yes I got laid! We both did! But I'm back now and I have the entire day here in the Big Apple and I'm taking a quick tour on one of those double decker busses. I wanted to let you know that I've arrived safely and I also wanted to ask you if... What? Yes hold on..."

A recording was telling Rebecca to drop in some more money if she wanted to continue. He wondered if she realized she had just answered a recording. After, apparently, dropping some money, Rebecca continued.

"Anyway where was I?...Oh yes, The thing is, I... I have to talk to you tonight. It's very important. You know that I have to return to work tomorrow, right away, because they give us so little vacation time, but if we don't talk tonight we may never have the chance again, because I may forget. I want to talk while it's fresh in my mind. So please think of a place we can go tonight for some coffee. A Starbuck's or Caribou Coffee or something like that, because it's important. I think there's a place at Crocker if I'm not mistaken and not in a big noisy restaurant please. We need to go to a place where people sit and read or chat. Well anyway I'll see you later then..."

There was a very long pause. More than fifteen seconds and he thought maybe that she had misplaced the receiver so that it was still off the hook. But then she spoke again, and her voice, for just three words, dropped, and she sounded like she was saying the most important thing ever said.

"It's about fate," she said, then back in her normal voice, "Okay, bye for real now, Julian. I love you." She hung up and Julian's answering machine said, in the clipped artificial voice of a computer female, "End. Of. Message."

What could she have meant about fate? he wondered. He played the message again but he couldn't discern any more meaning. He decided to make some eggs and a Bloody Mary and give himself a little more time to recover from his long night, before starting his laundry, but while cooking and eating; then sorting and washing and drying and folding and ironing, he continued to think about her fate comment. It took the place of his obsession about the threatening letter. And as the day wore on and he slogged his way through the various chores, including his weekly call to his mom and dad, who lived in Arizona near Sedona, facing a golf course (so that they didn't have to worry about keeping up a lawn, they said), he started to realize that there was something between Rebecca and himself that had been, for the most part, mostly harmless, he thought, but which he found today was actually quite awful.

He didn't know her.

He knew of her, of course — her mannerisms, her routine, her physiognomy. And he knew how she could stand around at any party and talk to everyone and make pleasant and sometimes confusing conversation. He knew her outline and shape, her height and her stance, her slight slouch and the slope of her shoulder, her gait and her chin and her glasses and her pony tail which she often stroked.

But he didn't really know her, did he? After all these years — almost ten. And he wondered about this all day. He was generally a simple person, he felt: a simple and well liked person. It was only around Rebecca that he ever thought himself "complicated," and that was because she often made him think about things that had never before occurred to him — like the 'talking while in motion' point she made awhile back. So he accepted her, just as she accepted him, but he wasn't really sure if he actually knew her.

On the way to the airport he developed this concocted image of Rebecca which he couldn't get out of his mind. It was as if a small version of Rebecca was standing on the hood of his car looking at him, her back to the wind, while he sped along Route 480. All she was doing in this image was giggling and constantly putting her hand up to her mouth to cover her laugh. She was, in his imagination, saying something without speaking it, and it seemed to be, "Oh Julian, silly, I've always been right here. I've always been right here in front of you."

While he waited for her plane to land, because he ended up arriving early and her plane ended up arriving late, he wondered what the image in his mind could actually mean. Rebecca was his best friend. He was a closeted homosexual and he couldn't afford to lose her. That was it. He couldn't afford to lose her, and he suddenly felt that not only could he lose her, but that he was also about to.

Chapter 20

They talked on the way to the coffee place at Crocker Park, but she had not said anything that seemed particularly important about fate. He had asked her about her trip and about "getting lucky" and she gave only a few vague answers. She said something about a swarthy South African man who had cunningly seduced her. When he asked her who else she had met on the trip she said, "oh a Belgian chocolate maker and an actress from some zombie movie." She laughed at a joke he didn't get and it was obvious to Julian the trip she had just taken wasn't really on her mind right now. There was something else.

"Do you know the expression, 'I heard it through the grapevine?'" she asked.

"Yes."

"Did you know it's from a bar in Greenwich Village? There was a bar called The Grapevine. People would ask, 'how did you hear about that' and they would say, 'Oh I heard it at The Grapevine'. And then somehow that became 'through the Grapevine' and now everyone says 'I heard it through the grapevine.'"

"And?"

"And nothing. I just thought it was an interesting bit of trivia. The bar was torn down fifty years ago but it still exists, in a different form. It's like an echo. A living echo."

Once they had purchased their coffees and desserts and were seated, she looked up at Julian and smiled. He smiled back.

"The plane ride was so long. It was worse on the way back. Nearly 18 hours and we had to stop on an island to refuel. But they let us get off to stretch our legs. They let us walk on the tarmac. I couldn't believe how big the plane was."

She appeared to look at the cashier, who was behind his back, then returned her gaze to him. "What I mean is that I had a lot of time to think," she said.

"About what?"

"About us. About me. My job. My father."

"Well... what about... all that?"

"I told you Principal Blount banned me from teaching about evolution didn't I?"

"No."

"Oh. Well he did. He said I'd lose my job."

"Well that sucks."

"I know." She paused and seemed, to his eyes, utterly unclear on what she was trying to say. But she was never unclear. This was a side to her he had never seen before. "I haven't been very happy," she finally said, looking down at her cup.

"Why?"

"For lots of reasons. Menopause. Principal Blount. Bruce when he called me a fag hag at your Thanksgiving dinner last year. My father dying of course. But it was really that put down Bruce made, that derogatory dismissal of me, that did it."

"But that's just Bruce. You can't listen to Bruce. Bruce is Bruce. What do you expect from someone who goes to the mall to shout things at old people? He's Bruce The Low for a reason. He's bitter and he hates living in Illyria and all the jokes are just to cover it up."

"I know. I know he's a clown. I know he's unhappy. But what he said still got me thinking about things."

Julian didn't know how to respond. "Like what things?" he finally asked. He took a bite of his cake to pretend that he wasn't nervous.

"Being single. Being your fag hag."

"I told you before you're not my fag hag. I hate that word. You're my best friend."

"Julian. There were eight men at your Thanksgiving dinner and one woman. Do you even know any other women?"

He couldn't deny that. She continued.

"But that's not what I was thinking about on the plane on the way back. On the plane I kept thinking about my Aunt Vicky and the way she's into genealogy and the four hundred years the Overs, or Overtons, have been in America and the way she tries to make that into something like American royalty. And then the way my father would literally fart whenever she tried to bring up the subject."

She and Julian both laughed. He remembered some event at her dad's house, probably Christmas, where her dad had actually popped some gas in the middle of her aunt's boring talk about their family background. He had always thought her father was kind of funny that way. But he had also been kind of intimidating. He had never told Rebecca either of those things.

"She thinks genetics gives her some sort of privilege which doesn't make sense because everyone who's living has ancestors that go back thirteen generations, or 100, or 1000. I know they don't believe in evolution anymore but even if you think the world is only 6000 years old it doesn't change the fact that we've all been living the same amount of time. We're all inheritors."

He enjoyed listening to Rebecca but he often became confused when she talked and this was one of those times. "What do you mean we're all inheritors?" he asked, as he took another bite of his cake to help him fake his part of the conversation.

"I mean we inherit the genes of our ancestors. We inherit their genes and traits, and we inherit their feelings. We inherit their behaviors. We inherit their intelligence and health and illness sometimes. And mental health and mental sickness, too. People forget about that. Vicky likes to think that only the noble and best qualities pass down, but so do the flaws. Anybody who looks into their background, in an honest way I mean, if they're able to, is going to find murderers and rapists and all sorts of nefarious characters."

"Makes sense," he said, but then he had a sudden image of Little Miss Myers again and the words "Drug Dealer" came into his mind. Of course. The purse with all that candy. He was their candy dealer. He was their future drug dealer. That's why they didn't attack him. Philip had already figured it out. His parents probably dealt pot to make some money.

"But what if someone was born, after all those years," Rebecca continued, "who was supposed to change all that. What if someone was born whose purpose it was to pay for all those crimes and felonies? To live a different life? To not pass it along. To put an end to it. Like Cleopatra."

It took him a moment to stop thinking about Philip and turn his attention back to Rebecca. "Sorry Rebecca, I don't know what you're talking about."

"That's the problem. Neither do I," she laughed and took a long gulp of her coffee. "I shouldn't be drinking coffee at this hour. I guess what I'm saying is that I saw all these animals who were living their lives... ummm... I don't know how to put it... outside the law. Lawless. Like we saw a clan of hyenas rip apart this baby Impala and devour it."

"Oh my God."

"Oh Julian it was so horrible. It was the most awful thing I've ever seen in my life. This woman from California actually had to be sent home she was so upset. And we saw an elephant give birth."

"Are you kidding?"

"No. I'm not. And everything... I don't know how to put it... but it all seemed so human to me. Everything looked human." Her eyes started to well.

"Rebecca?"

A tear fell down one of her cheeks and she quickly wiped it away as if she was embarrassed. "Sorry. I guess I'm trying to say that I think I can forgive myself now."

"For what?"

"For everything." She shook her head when she said this and smiled. Julian frowned because that sounded like an infantile evasion, but he didn't push it. She reached across and took his hand in hers. "And I just wanted to tell you that no matter what happens, I will always be here for you. Always."

She was smiling and her gaze was very intense. He thought about telling her about his threatening letter but he had the feeling she wasn't done. And he was a little afraid to bring it up.

"I'll always be here for you," she said again, and then added, very emphatically, "just as long as you never look in the basket." She let go of his hand.

"Basket?" he asked. "What basket. Did you buy a basket in Botswana? Why can't I see it?"

"Never mind," she said, waving it away with her hand. "It was just a joke my South African seducer told me."

"Oooh," he said, grateful to be getting on to more real-world topics, "you still haven't told me about him. Was he nice looking?"

"Oh very. He was wonderful. His balls were the size of small grapefruits."

"Rebecca!"

"Oh please Julian, don't turn prudish. Anyway I'll tell you all about it in the car. Let's go. I've still got to unpack and get ready for my kids tomorrow. Plus I want to cut this off." She indicated her pony tail.

"No Rebecca, you can't. I know I tease you about it but that's your comfort. Why do you want to cut it off?"

"It's old," she said, "it's time I got rid of the old things in my life."

He didn't tell her this, but he was left with the disturbing feeling that she was talking about him.

Chapter 21

Julian took the last bite of his cake and was, on the way out, about to start telling her the story of his threatening letter, when he suddenly had the strange feeling that they had switched social positions, and that she was in possession of all the confidence he had felt himself losing since receiving the letter. It was as if she was going to start having dinner parties which he would attend. He found that he was a bit embarrassed to bring it up, so he didn't right away.

But once in the car, with his attention taken by the road and in the dim light of the dashboard, he was finally able to tell her about the letter. She was outraged, and her outrage made him feel better and more secure. He parked his car in the parking lot of her apartment building, and they talked about the letter for another fifteen minutes. They discussed what to do about it, and what it could have meant, whether it could have been sent by Philip, and whether or not to report it. Rebecca, because she was very well read, remembered that ink jet printers leave a miniature yellow identity code — nearly invisible to the naked eye — that most people didn't know about and with her trusty magnifying glass they would be able to read this code if, that is, it was printed on a color ink jet printer. And that was all they could do about it at the moment. But it was enough to make Julian feel hopeful again.

After they talked about the letter, Julian helped carry Rebecca's luggage into her apartment where she discovered she had left the urn with her father's ashes right there on her dining table, which gave her a huge laugh. Finally, back out by his car, he said he was glad she was back and had a good time and he gave her a hug goodbye, a hug that for some reason, he wanted to prolong.

As he was driving home, and thinking about their friendship which seemed, for no reason he could discern, to be winding down, some vague memories about Rebecca came to him along the way prompted by the urn she had left on the table. Primarily it was the weird way she had suddenly wanted to go to Africa to spread her father's ashes there. And then why she had insisted upon cremating her father in the first place when it had caused such a huge fight with her aunt. He remembered asking Rebecca if it was her father's wish to be cremated and she had answered, strangely, that her father didn't believe he could die.

But she had said it like... like what? "My father didn't think he could die." It sounded like something you would say if you had won. But won what? And then she was complaining about her aunt again, her Aunt Vicky who she called, "the genealogist." She was causing a lot of trouble apparently, going on and on about getting an autopsy for her brother because she kept insisting that he was getting better, whatever that meant. That was silly, Rebecca said, because he had pancreatic cancer and almost no one survives. "But why don't you just let them do an autopsy just to put your aunt's mind at ease," he asked, and she had said, "I can't," and then it was all over anyway, the new school year started and he forgot about all of that Over family drama. But then he remembered, as he made a right turn onto Crestwood, two minutes from his little house, that she had laughed once and said, in a highly affected British accent, "Oh Julian darling, maybe I ought to just kill my Aunt Vicky, she's really starting to enrage me and she is, after all, a crashing bore. I could sprinkle some pentobarbital on a baked potato and the whole damn drama would be over and done."

And as he pulled up into his driveway he remembered that until he died, Rebecca had said her father was improving every time he asked. But then he suddenly died. But why would she have done that? He couldn't believe that she would do such a thing. No it was absolutely impossible, just impossible; one of those strange fantasies people occasionally have about their friends: like what if she was a CIA operative, or what if he was a terrorist, or what if she murdered her father? And because she was a woman, he decided, it was actually just one of those mysterious things about women that men never understand, like how they can be fighting one minute, then braiding each other's hair the next.

So Julian got out of his car and put the horrible thought out of his mind, and after he closed his garage door and disappeared into his house, he never thought about it, ever again.

Chapter 22

"Philip please sit down," Rebecca said, "and please put your purse under your seat like the girls have to do until the class is over. You know you don't have special privileges."

"But Miss Over," Philip said, "what if someone tries to steal it?"

"I'm standing right here in front of you Philip I can see everything that happens."

"Not everything," Philip said defiantly, as he sat. He had his usual tiny grin, she noticed.

"Not everything what?" Rebecca asked.

"Not everything Miss Over."

"Yes, Philip, everything. I see everything. I see everything that happens in this room. And if you're worried about your purse you should stop bringing it, and all the candy in it, to school."

Philip, while she waited with her hands on her hips, carefully placed his purse on the wire rack underneath his seat. Once he had, she said to the class, "Now I'm going to tell all of you a story. And I want you to try to remember this story, because it's a very old story that comes from Africa. And after I'm done telling it, I want all the girls to get together on the right side of the room and talk about what the story means, and I want all the boys to get together and move to the left side of the room and do the same."

The eagerness in their eyes was obvious. People love stories. They tell stories and they love stories. Something about being human that makes it almost a requirement, to tell stories. To tell stories about what happened.

But Philip Myers, who was, oddly enough, her most difficult and disruptive student, raised his hand to ask another pointless question. She knew he used his questions to harass her but she had not, so far, found a way of stifling him and she refused to resort to shame which was, shockingly, something she frequently wanted to do to make him shut the hell up.

"Yes Philip?" Rebecca asked.

"Which side do you want me to go to Miss Over?"

"You'll go to the boy's side," she answered, without hesitation.

Although he didn't look pleased, he seemed to accept her decision without contesting it. She remembered wanting to make Philip her pet when Julian had first told her about him, but when he reached her level, he had turned out to be a hateful little creep she wanted to strangle. Until Philip, she had never disliked a student.

He scoffed at her and he made her feel old and out of it and made her not only question her abilities as a teacher but made her feel like one of those people that everyone thinks has never enjoyed life. He made her glad that she had never had children.

But she still had a job to do and the job included Philip. She would have this job until retirement, having decided not to sell her father's home but moving into it and making it her own. It might have been a nice pot of money to finance another trip to see the polar bears, or to retire early, but she liked the garden in the back and she had expanded it from the tiny plot her father had kept. She thought about her father's ashes in it — both halves now, and the fish tank ashes in the official cemetery where her aunt went every anniversary to leave flowers. She was pleased that all his ashes ended up in the dirt in her backyard, in her garden, growing up into the plants and flowers and the young evergreen she had planted.

Sometimes, when working in her garden, she would stop and sit back on her heels and think about her trip to Africa, and she would think about that extraordinary scene she acted out with the hippo, where she dared it to kill her, thinking that her father was "in" it. She told no one about it, not even David. She wondered at the time if the hippo was her "judge," but then months later she wondered if it had been Marcel DeKoning all along. He had created what turned out to be the most beautiful picture of her that she ever had taken. She usually looked like a silly dork in people's pictures, with one eye half shut or her mouth open in the middle of a sentence. But the picture Marcel took, which she now proudly hung in her living room was about 2-½ feet tall. In it, she was standing in a Botswanan canoe in front of a large clutch of Papyrus reeds which formed a gorgeous dark green backdrop to her pinkish face and a thick white bathrobe, a robe that had been supplied by the actress since they were about the same height and the star had forgiven her by that morning.

Whatever it was — the star's robe or the papyrus background or Marcel's skill or the flowers Elizabeth DeKoning had put in her hair — she looked as peaceful and as content and majestic as she had ever looked in her life. She almost looked like a queen herself, standing there in white, in front of the green papyrus staring off at something distance. When she first unwrapped it she nearly cried, not only because she was so beautiful in the picture but also because it had been taken by that annoying man.

And when she started seeing David Miller, the funeral home director, it turned out to be an unexpectedly easy conversation starter, because she could always add something more about it. It had actually helped them ease their way into a relationship, one which seemed to be going nicely. The photograph seemed to balance everything.

But sometimes, here in the classroom, in the real world where problems exist and have to be taken care of, she wondered if it wasn't Philip who was her secret judge. It always seemed like he was trying to scare her.

But if a giant hippo didn't scare her then neither would this child, so once the class was settled and Philip's need to mock her was sated, she told the story which she now used as a substitute for what used to be a short discussion of evolution. Last year it had been an enjoyable and unusual experience: the boys coming up with a meaning to the story that was almost exactly the opposite of what the girls had read into it. She had asked the class to come up with an answer to the question, "What was in the basket?" The boys answered "nothing." The girls answered "everything." It was the most startling thing that had ever happened in one of her classrooms. So she had decided to tell this ancient story every year in place of evolution. At least until someone came along and told her she had to teach the children that the universe was created by a very intelligent space alien.

This was the story she told:

Once there was a little fellow, she said, *whose name was Khoi Khoi, and he was a short black fellow with high cheek bones and good teeth and eyes. But he was sad because he was poor. He had no money to buy food and no money to gamble with his friends. He would spend the whole day crying into his hands and feeling sorry for himself.*

One day, another man named Heiseb was walking down the road and he walked by Khoi-khoi's home and saw him sitting on a log at the side of his house, crying into his hands. So Heiseb decided to give him a herd of six beautiful healthy cows which produced the best milk for hundreds of miles around. And he gave them to Khoi-khoi and told him to stop crying because these cows would bring him great wealth, happiness and love for the rest of his life. And Khoi-khoi was very happy and said "thank you Heiseb," and Heiseb left the cows with Khoi-khoi and went along on his way. But Heiseb could not hide his laughter, and Khoi-khoi wondered why Heiseb was laughing, but he soon forgot about it.

Khoi-khoi's cows had smooth brown hides and they were eager to be milked every day. They were so eager to be milked they would flick their tails up in the air, like mailboxes, so that Khoi-khoi would know they needed milking. And for awhile Khoi-khoi was a very happy fellow. He sang little songs and did little dances, and boasted to all his friends that he had the best cows in the land.

But one morning, Khoi-khoi woke to discover that none of his cows flipped their tails up when the saw him approaching, and when he sat down to milk them he discovered why. It was because they had already been milked.

He went all over the place looking for the person who milked his cows, but he couldn't find the bandit who had done it.

The next morning, when he approached the cows, they didn't flip their tails up and so again, he walked all over the place, but he couldn't find the bandit who had done it.

So that night he stayed up all night and carried a leather whip called a sjambok and hid behind a bush near the cows so he could give the thief a good sound beating.

He waited for a long while and nothing happened. But then the moon rose, and as soon as she began to shine and covered everything in her silky light, down from the stars fell a golden rope, and down this golden rope came seven young girls, who were all born from the stars. And six of the girls carried empty milk pails, while the seventh carried a basket. These were the girls that were coming down at night to steal the milk of his cows. So Khoi-khoi jumped up from his hiding place and swung the sjambok over his head and screamed "ayiiii" and all the girls screamed and raced back to the rope to climb back up to the stars. And the first six girls with the milking pots got away, but the seventh girl, the girl with the basket, didn't have enough time to make it up the rope, and just as she was about to start climbing, Khoi-khoi caught her by the foot and pulled her back down. And then the rope disappeared into the stars as the other girls pulled it back, leaving the seventh girl stranded below.

Now of all seven girls, this one was the prettiest and the youngest. She was just fourteen years old, and the basket she carried was made of very tightly knotted sisal. It had a large body, and it was fitted with a very tight cover.

The beautiful young girl hid the basket behind her body. Khoi-khoi asked her to show him, but she looked down at the ground and refused. Then he said he had been very lonely and would marry her so that he wouldn't be lonely anymore. And he said that he would make her till the fields as punishment for stealing his milk. The young girl replied that she would be happy to marry him, but only on the condition that he never look inside the basket. He thought about this for a moment, and then he agreed to never look inside the basket. And they were married.

Things were splendid for Khoi-khoi and his wife, and the cows continued to produce their rich milk and lifted their tails when they needed milking. The wife he captured tilled the fields every day, without complaint, and Khoi-khoi did as he promised, and never opened the basket. And they were very happy together and they grew to love each other.

One day, after many years had passed, Khoi-khoi's curiosity overcame him. And he decided that he had to know what was inside the basket. So while his wife was out tilling the fields, he took the basket from the corner where she had put it, and he blew away the sand and dust that covered it, and he pulled on the lid and he managed to pry the lid off. But when he looked inside the basket, he saw that the basket was completely empty. There was nothing in it at all. So he laughed and laughed and said to himself, "She is such a stupid woman, my wife." He put the cover back on the basket and he put the basket in the corner, and he sat on his big log beside the house and had a smoke and waited for his wife to return from the fields with a big smile on his face.

And it just so happened, that Heiseb happened to walk down the road. He waved and shouted at Khoi-khoi and said, "Are you still happy with the cows?" And Khoi-khoi said, "Yes Heiseb, thank you very much for giving them to me," and Heiseb laughed and continued on his way.

Now when his wife came from the fields, she saw Khoi-khoi sitting on his big log, beside his house, and as soon as she saw him smiling to himself and nodding his head with satisfaction she knew what he had done. She knew that he had looked inside the basket and she started to weep. Tears streamed down her face, and she covered her eyes with her hands and sank to the ground in a small bundle. When Khoi-khoi saw her he got up from his big log and walked over to her and shouted down at her and said, "Why are you crying you stupid woman?"

She said, "Because you broke your promise and looked in the basket."

"Yes," Khoi-khoi admitted, "I looked in the basket. So what?"

She wiped the tears from her cheeks and from where she sat on the ground, looked up at him for a moment, before asking the question that she had to ask.

"What did you see?" she asked.

"Nothing," he said.

And right before his eyes, she vanished.

The End

Thomas F. Cook is a writer and amateur photographer who has lived in New York for 30 years writing plays, screenplays, and more recently, novels. He has worked variously as a telephone pollster, knife salesman, typist, and computer geek. This is his second novel.